KANE

SUSIE MCIVER

KANE
BAND OF NAVY SEALS

BOOK SEVEN

**AUTHOR
SUSIE MCIVER**

This is a work of fiction. Names, characters, organizations, places, events, and incidents are either products of the author's imagination or are used fictitiously.

Text copyright 2021 Suise McIver

All rights reserved.

No part of this book may be reproduced, or stored in a retrieval system, or transmitted in any form or by any means, electronic, mechanical, photocopying, recording or otherwise, without express written permission of the author.

Cover Design by Emmy Ellis

❦ Created with Vellum

1

KANE

Kane was not happy. He'd been lying on his stomach in the damn icy slush for almost two hours. If the guy didn't show up in the next ten minutes, he was leaving. This entire situation was strange. He had a text on his phone to go there and wait until someone showed up with a kidnapped girl. Kane didn't know who sent the message. He had a feeling it was from Julia but it was only a feeling. Given the fact that his mind was consumed by her, he wasn't sure whether his feelings could be trusted. He missed Julia, the only woman he's ever loved. The woman who dropped him when he told her he loved her. He had to stop himself from thinking about her all the time. She had wavy brunette hair that hung down her back. Her eyes were as blue as the sea. When she smiled at him, his heart would beat so fast he used to think he would have a heart attack. Julia was perfect. She worked out every day. Kane used to work out with her before she refused to see him. Just because he told her, he loved her.

He refocused on what he was doing. Kane had been staring at the damn cabin like it was going to disappear. He was about to get up and leave when he heard a noise. Holding his breath, he tried to keep his teeth from chattering. It was frigging cold out there in the mountains. Suddenly, it sounded like there was a scuffle. Kane looked through the trees but couldn't see anything. Then he heard a man shouting at someone, breaking the silence.

"I told you to shut the fuck up. If you don't stop fighting me, I'm going to have to hurt you again. Is that what you want?" he menaced. "Why do I always take these damn jobs? I'm not allowed to screw you, but I can beat you. That's pretty damn stupid. I believe I'm going to ignore that order."

Kane watched as he pushed the girl inside the cabin and she fell to the floor. Kane tried standing, but his legs were numb from the wet, frozen slush. He did a few leg bends before his legs worked good enough to kick the door open. He could have made a lot of noise and not be heard. The girl was screaming, and the man was swearing loud enough to not hear anything. When Kane kicked the door open, the man turned with a knife in his hand. Kane lunged at him kicking it out of his hand. He knocked him out and put zipties on his arms and legs in what seemed like seconds. Once done, Kane stood up and looked at the girl.

She was a skinny little thing, by what he could see in the dark cabin. She was frightened, and she looked like she was going to make a dash for the door. Kane held his hands up. "I'm here to help you, don't be afraid."

"How did you know I was going to be here?"

"I didn't know you were going to be here. I had a text saying a girl is going to need my help. I was given the address, and I've waited a few hours in that icy slush for you to show up. So do you want to tell me what the hell is going on?"

"This man took me from my mother. He shot her and grabbed me," she told him. Her chin wobbled. "My father will kill him and his friends for killing my mother and kidnapping me," the girl said. She tried to fight the urge to break down.

"How do you know he has friends?"

"Because they dropped us off at the edge of the forest. They were going to hide the car," she replied. The realization that they could be close made her panic. "We have to go now. Someone is supposed to come and get me from here," she continued. Tears fell unheeded down her face and her emotions got hold of her, "Why did they have to kill her?"

Kane knew there was nothing he could say to soothe her pain. "It'll be alright, lass. I'm here now. Just because your mom was shot doesn't mean she's dead. I've been shot before, and I'm still here. A buddy of mine was shot seven times, and he lived. So keep good thoughts. Listen, we need to get the hell out of here. Do you have shoes?"

"No, they took me from our house and I didn't have my shoes on."

Kane took the boots off of the man and tied them real tight so they wouldn't slip off the girl. Then he took the guy's jacket off. To do that, he had to cut the ties off. Kane worked fast and had the ties back on in a couple of seconds. "Come on, I'll call the police when we are further away from the cabin. Then you can contact your father."

"Okay, I won't let them catch me. I'm not real strong right now. I used to be. But I've been sick."

Kane looked at her. "If you feel like you are going to slow down, and if you let me, I can carry you. I don't want these guys catching us. My vehicle is about a mile away."

"I don't care if you carry me. I don't think I can walk or run right now."

Kane turned and picked her up and flung her over his left shoulder. "Hang on to me. I'm going to cut through these trees. We need to get as far away from these people as we can. What's your name?"

"Riley."

"Okay, Riley, here we go," he said. Kane ran until he saw lights ahead. They couldn't be hunting for them already, could they? "Don't say a thing. I see some lights up ahead. What kind of vehicle were you in?"

"An SUV. Don't forget someone was going to pick me up from there. So it could be their car."

"Yeah, that's right. Let me see if I can see anything," he replied. Kane looked at the vehicle as it slowed down. Then they turned the lights out. *Why did they turn off the headlights? Do they know we are out here?* Kane wasn't going to risk Riley's life. He headed for his vehicle, listening for any noise he could hear. He thought he heard a shout, so he ran the rest of the way to his truck. He put Riley in the passenger side and jumped behind the wheel.

"Call Ryes," Kane said out loud to his vehicle. He could hear the ringing.

"Hello?"

"Rye's, I need your help. I just rescued a girl, her name is Riley. She said the guys who kidnapped her shot her mom. She is going to give you her address," Kane reported. He looked over at Riley as he kept his foot on the gas pedal sending the car flying down the back road.

"Hello, Riley, you can go ahead and give me the information."

"Hello, we live in Malibu. Eight-eight-eight-one-three, Carrigan Road. Can you call my dad too? His phone number is four-two-two five-one-one-three."

"You don't want to call him?"

"I don't think I can. I'm going to be sick," she replied. Riley looked at Kane. "Sorry."

The poor lass started vomiting, then she had the dry

heaves. "Here lass, take this bottle of water and wet this cloth. You'll feel better after you wipe your face off," he told her. His car phone rang. "Hello."

"I want to talk to my daughter."

"Daddy," Riley cried.

"Riley, thank God, you're okay."

"They killed Mama."

"No, no, honey, your mom is going to be okay. We were so scared for you. Here's your mother, she wants to say something."

"Riley, are you okay darling? Did those men hurt you?" she asked. Her voice was weak but she was very much alive.

"Mama, I thought they killed you. Tell Daddy those men want to kill him."

As if she didn't hear a word, she muttered, "Everything is going to be okay. Here's Daddy."

"Riley, I want you to listen to Kane. He's going to help you. We are all going to a safe house. Kane will bring you to where we are. We'll see you in a little while. We love you, Riley."

"I love you too."

It got real quiet. Kane noticed the lass thinking. She didn't say anything, but he knew she wanted to say something. "What's on your mind?"

"Since I became sick, my parents think we need to live near the hospital. My dad helped to catch some cartel people, and they must have found him. That's why those men wanted me. I'm sure they wanted to trade me for my dad. This scares me. We've moved three times before I got sick. Now my parents are afraid to move because of me."

"I'm sorry you've been sick. Can I ask what your sickness is?"

"I had meningitis. I don't have it anymore, so you don't have to worry about catching it. It's taking longer to get well than it should. My parents keep taking me to the hospital to see what's wrong with me. I should be completely healed but I can't seem to get well."

"How old are you?"

"I'm twenty-two."

"Are you? I would have guessed you were fourteen or fifteen. But then again, I haven't seen you in the light. I'm sorry we have to drive in the dark until we get away from this area."

"Well, since you have only seen me in the dark, I'm ordinary-looking. I don't have any special features. My mouth is too big, and my eyes are goldish in color. Sometimes they turn greenish. I do have black eyelashes. I do look younger than twenty-two. My hair is cute, I guess. The girl who cut it said it was," Riley said and chuckled. "I bought some wine once, and the guy lectured me for having a fake I.D. He wouldn't believe me when I said I was twenty-one."

"Now you got me curious."

"Are my parents where I'm going?"

"Yes, they are. Like your dad said, they'll be in a safe house that we own. We have safe houses all over the United States. I'm not sure which one you and your family will be staying in yet but a call will come through soon to let me know or something," Kane explained. He saw her yawn. "If you're tired, you can rest your eyes. We have at least an hour to go."

"Okay, thank you," Riley said, shutting her eyes. The truck was nice and cozy except for the vomit. "I'll clean your truck out," she whispered as she drifted off to sleep.

2

*K*ane pulled into one of the six garages at the safe house. When the garage door closed, a man and woman ran out of the house and into the garage. The woman was crying and holding her arm that was in a sling. Kane kept the doors locked until he saw Rowan, who nodded. When he opened Riley's door, she woke up. Kane smiled as he got his first look at her. She had blue hair and gold-green eyes. She smiled at Kane.."

He chuckled. "Hello, Riley. You're beautiful."

"Hello, Kane. Thank you. These are my parents, Jerry and Stephanie Kaiser. Riley's dad pulled her into his arms. I'm so sorry, honey; this was all my fault. I should have hired men to guard you and your mom. I didn't realize how much revenge these men wanted."

"Mama, I thought you were dead."

"No, they shot me in the arm. It must have scared me, and I passed out. When I woke up, you were gone. I freaked out and called your dad and the police," she said. Stephanie looked at Kane "How did you know about Riley?" she asked him.

"I was having dinner with a lady when I got a text that said a teenager needed my help. The text told me where to go. It said for me to leave right then. So I apologized to the lady and left. I need to take a shower, and Riley needs to soak in a warm tub."

Riley looked down at herself. "I don't have any clothes here."

"We'll get you something to wear," Kane said, trying to see where Rowan had taken off to. "Did you see…?"

Before he could finish his sentence, a noise at the back door had him turning with his gun pointed at the love of his life. Too bad she didn't want to admit that she loved him too. Instead, she refused to be with him. All because he loved her. Right now, she looked angry, as she headed straight for Jerry Kaiser.

"What the fuck is wrong with you. I told you to move your family. Did you not take me seriously? Why didn't you leave?" she asked, serious. Julia closed her eyes and counted to three. That's as far as she allowed herself. She looked around at the people standing there: the woman, the girl who was actually a young lady, and Kane. She would give anything to be with Kane again, to sleep in his arms whenever she felt like it, but it wasn't meant to be. She loved him whispering in her ear with that Scottish voice of his. When they made love, she could barely understand him. His brogue would become so thick. He was handsome with all that black hair and green eyes. He was everything she ever wanted. Julia took a deep breath and looked at the girl. She smiled at the young lady. "I'm sorry for yelling at your father. I'm really nothing like that," Julia apologized. She heard Kane and Jerry smirk but decided to ignore them. Instead, she focused on Riley, who didn't look well.

Then she looked at Jerry. "So have you decided that's it's to your advantage to go into hiding?"

"Julia, we have gone into hiding. But Riley is sick, and they know it. I believe someone at the hospital is telling them when she comes in, and they followed us home."

"Of course, they did," Julia turned to Riley, "what's wrong with you?"

"I had meningitis. I just haven't been able to get my health back."

Kane took a deep breath. "Can we talk later? I've been lying in icy slush for hours. I need a shower, and Riley needs a good soaking. Riley, I'll get you one of my T-shirts to wear. Maybe there are some sweats around here that you could put on. I'll call Austin and see if he knows of any. Damn, he's been gone a year already. When the hell is he coming back? Follow me, Riley, and I'll show you where the tub is," Kane said. He looked at Jerry "Did someone tell you where to sleep?"

"Yes, we are all taken care of. Julia, I would like to speak to you."

"I'm sorry, I don't have time," she replied then turned and walked out the back door.

Kane shook his head. "Why are you leaving through the back door?"

"I don't want to be seen."

Kane shook his head, "Who would see you?" She kept walking.

Kane walked upstairs. Even though he had his own home, he'd been staying here most of the time since most of the Seals were married. Four more of his ex-Navy Seal buddies would be arriving next week. He got a T-shirt for Riley and took it to the room she'd be staying in. Then he went back to his room and stripped out of his wet clothes. When he stepped under the shower, it felt like heaven. That was until Julia's image popped in his head. He wished he could stop loving her, but she was the only woman he'd ever loved. He got out of the shower and went to find something to eat. He missed dinner and was starving. He decided to have a fried ham and egg sandwich. As he was cooking his egg, Riley walked into the kitchen.

"I bet you are hungry. Neither one of us had dinner. You take this sandwich, and I'll make another one."

"Awesome, thank you. I haven't been eating much since I've been sick. But this smells delicious."

"You need to eat more. That will help you with all the health problems you have going on right now. I'll help you. If you want to stay here, you can. I cook all the time."

"You will? My parents don't say a lot about me eating. I think they are afraid to upset me. They watch me every second. It kind of freaks me out. I want to tell them to stop, but I also don't want to upset them. Thank you for bringing us here. This is the first time my dad has actually gone to bed and gone to sleep in a long time. Mom said he went to sleep as soon as his head hit the pillow."

"Has he left the FBI?"

"He's not FBI. He's DEA. I don't think he's left them. It's just that he's been worried about us, so he's taken time off."

"He's DEA? I'll call my friend Lucas tomorrow and let him know what's going on."

"Is that Lucas Ryan?"

"Yeah, do you know him?"

"Yes, I haven't seen him since I was about sixteen. He always seemed angry to me. He's my dad's friend."

"Yeah he used to be angry all the time. Until he married Skye. Now he's happy. Did you like your sandwich?"

Riley looked at her plate, and the sandwich was gone. She laughed. "It was delicious."

Kane gave her another one. "Are you still in school?"

"Yes, I'm a senior in college; I've been doing my schooling

online. I need to get my computer and some things from my house."

"We'll worry about that tomorrow. I'm sure your house is being watched. I'm going to head up to bed. Make yourself at home here. But don't go outside. The alarms are crazy loud."

"Okay, thank you."

Kane walked upstairs, thinking about Julia. If he could go back, he never would have told Julia he loved her. He would have waited until she didn't ever want to be away from him. Julia liked everyone to think she was all tough, but he knew how gentle she really was. He knew she had strong feelings for him when Rory, his sister, was in the hospital, and they didn't know if she would live or not. Julia came to the hospital to be with him. She stayed there until the doctor said Rory would live. Julia didn't say anything to him about the two of them, and he wasn't allowed to say anything to her about them either. Their love was hidden from everyone while they were together. Julia didn't want anyone to know they were in a relationship. So for the six months they dated, he never told his friends, and Julia never told her friends.

A couple of his buddies knew about them. Kane didn't know how they found out, and he didn't care. The only persons he talked to about him and Julia were his sisters. When his grandfather died, he went back to Scotland. He and Rory had a few shots of whiskey together. Rory could drink almost anyone under the table. Kane ended up spilling his guts after a few shots of whiskey and some perfectly timed questions from Rory. Then she had to tell their sister Elspeth he was in love with someone named Julia Sparrow.

Kane took a cold shower and went to bed. He was exhausted. This was a long day, and to see Julia at the end of it shook him up. He wondered why the cartel was after Jerry Kaiser. They might have to put them in a different safe house. They would all decide tomorrow morning at the meeting they were having.

3

*K*ane could smell coffee and bacon as he came down the stairs. Someone was cooking breakfast. He walked into the kitchen, and his sister Rory was there cooking. "Why are you here this early?"

"Jonah had lawyer stuff to do, so I came with him to visit you. I knew the way to get you downstairs was to cook breakfast."

"You look happy. What's that smile for?"

Rory set the spatula down and turned to Kane. "I'm having a baby. Can you believe I'm going to be a mother? What if I don't know what to do? I'm scared."

Kane picked her up and swung her around. You're going to be a wonderful mom. I'm so happy for you. When that baby gets here, you'll know exactly what to do. That's what Bird told me. She said it comes naturally."

"Thank you. I am so happy," she said. Rory turned back to the stove when she noticed movement out of the corner of her eye. She turned and smiled. "Hello."

"Hi."

. . .

"Riley, this is my sister Rory. She just told me I'm going to be an uncle."

"Congratulations."

"Thank you," Rory said. Come over here and take a chair. I have breakfast ready for you."

Riley sat down. "I don't usually eat breakfast."

"Oh. It would hurt my feelings if you didn't eat at least a little."

Kane was already digging in. He looked at Riley. "You don't want to hurt Rory's feelings. She's pregnant. She may start crying."

"I'm sorry, of course, I'll eat. It looks delicious."

"It is," Kane said, handing her a biscuit slathered with butter and honey.

He smiled at Rory when Riley ate that biscuit and took another one, slathering it with butter and honey herself. Rory got up and poured Riley a glass of orange juice. "Help yourself to some more. I always cook way too much," she told her.

"This is delicious. And I could listen to you and Kane talk forever. It makes me want to go to Scotland, and I've never been there."

"Oh, you have to go. It's beautiful; everything is so green. I miss taking long walks. I used to walk everywhere I went. My husband had the land behind our house landscaped like my homeland. Everything is green."

"One day, I will go. I promise that's one country I will visit," she said. Riley looked at Kane. "I have class this morning. Would it be alright if I go and get some of my things?"

"You can't leave here. But we'll get your things as soon as everyone is up. Why are they not up?"

"They left," Rory said, taking a drink of her orange juice.

"What do you mean? Who left?"

"Rowan took Riley's parents to another safe house."

"Do they want Kane to bring me to them?"

"Kane will have to call Rowan. I have no idea what they are doing."

Kane took out his phone and dialed Rowan's cell. He picked up on the first ring. "Hey, Rowan, where are you taking Riley's parents?"

"We are going to separate them. When Riley needs to go to the hospital, one of us will take her. But from now on, she'll go to a different hospital."

"I think that's a good idea. I'll let Riley know what's going on. She needs her computer for school and her clothes."

"Ryes and Julia went over there. They should be back there any time now."

"Why is Julia involved in this?"

"Because this was her case. The cartel found out Jerry was a DEA and went after him. Julia warned him three times to move away. He moved, and you know the story from there. Frankie is coming over this morning to check Riley."

"Okay, who is going to guard Jerry and Stephanie?"

"Luke Wilson is with them. Hunter Brown is on his way there. I'm going home. I'll talk to you later."

"Okay, I'll talk to you later," he replied. Kane looked at Riley. "Your parents are at another safe house. You'll stay here with us. Julia and Ryes have gone to your house to pack your things and bring them here."

"So my parents aren't going to be here with me?"

"No, does that bother you?"

Riley shook her head. "No, I know I'm going to sound ungrateful for them taking such good care of me while I've been sick. But they both smother me. I feel like they watch every breath I take. My mom and dad are so scared I'm going to die. Does that sound mean?"

"Not at all."

"Did your parents smother you?" she asked. First, she looked at Kane, then Rory.

Kane shook his head. "No, our parents died in an accident along with our grandmother when we were young. Our wonderful grandfather raised us."

"I'm sorry."

"We had a great life growing up. No reason to be sorry," he replied. Kane heard the garage door closing. "I think Julia and Ryes are here," Kane said. Ryes walked in carrying two suitcases.

"Hello, these must belong to you," Ryes said. He looked at the table. "Is there any breakfast left?"

"Yes, I put the food in the oven."

Riley smiled at the three of them. "Thank you, Rory. I swear you are the best cook."

Kane chuckled. "That's what you told me."

Riley giggled and stood up. "Both of you are great cooks," Riley replied. She looked at Ryes. "Thank you for getting these things for me. Is my computer in here also?"

"No, I have your computer right here," Julia said, walking into the kitchen, carrying two bags.

Julia stopped as she saw Riley wearing Kane's T-shirt. She knew it was his, as she'd taken it off of him before. Pain slammed into her heart, and water rushed to her eyes. *What the hell is the matter with me? This poor girl is sick. Why am I jealous? I'm the one who ended this relationship with Kane. I had no choice. Everyone who has ever loved me has died. I will not be responsible for the man I love dying.*

Kane saw the pain on Julia's face. "Julia, are you alright, sweetheart?"

"What? Yes, I'm alright. Here you go, Riley. How are you feeling?"

"I actually feel much better. Thank you both for getting

my things for me. Now I have to get to class," Riley said. Ryes followed her, carrying her bags.

Kane turned to Julia. She blinked her eyes to get rid of the moisture. "Rory, this is Julia Sparrow. Julia, this is my sister Rory."

"Hello, Julia."

"Hi, Rory. I'm so happy you are better. Kane was so worried about you."

"Thank you. I know he was. I'll try to stay away from flying bullets," she joked. Rory thought neither of them heard her. "Well, if you will excuse me, I'm going to call Jonah and see what time he's picking me up," Rory said, stepping away from the table.

It was just Kane and Julia standing in the kitchen. "Julia."

"Yes."

"Can we please talk?"

"I have to leave. I have to contact Juan in two hours."

"Juan. Are you talking about the damn cartel Juan?"

"Yes."

"When are you going to stop trying to kill yourself? You told me two years ago you would stop taking on these assignments."

"I know these people. Should I let someone who doesn't know anything about the cartel do my job? Someone who could get killed for not knowing if they were saying the right thing? I know these people, Kane. They know me. To them, I'm Sonya Skittle. Someone who knows what she's doing. They trust me. I don't want to be responsible for a newbie dying again."

"You can't take care of every new FBI agent."

"I did leave. Just like I said I would. Michelle Harris was sent in. She was undercover. She lasted three days. Three fucking days before they killed her. So what would you have me do?"

"Send a seasoned man in. It doesn't have to be a woman. You promised me you would quit. You can't break a promise just because you no longer want us to be together"

"I didn't say I wanted us to be apart. I said we had to because you said you loved me."

"So, are you saying if I take back the, I love you part, then we can start seeing each other again?"

"Do you still love me?"

"Do you love me?"

"I have to go," she replied. Julia grabbed a biscuit off the table and turned around. Kane caught her arm. He turned her around to face him.

He leaned his forehead against hers. "I wish like hell I didn't love you, but I do," he told her. Then he held her face in both hands and kissed her like it would be their last kiss. Kane knew Julia had issues about loving anyone, but he couldn't help how he felt about her. "How can I just turn off my feelings?" he asked.

"I don't know," she answered. Julia stepped back and turned around and left."

Rory wiped her eyes. "I'm sorry I overheard your conversation. I was afraid that if I moved, then Julia would hurry and leave before you were finished speaking. I wonder why she's so scared to let someone love her."

"So, you think Julia's afraid of me loving her? That could be true, but I can't take it back. I do love her. I'm not going to lie and tell her I don't."

"No, you can't do that. You should talk to Skye. She adopted Julia when she was fifteen.That's been some years back now. She probably knows her better than anyone."

"Yeah, I'll give her a call and see if I can talk to her. I better go check on Riley."

"She's doing school work. I was just in there. Thank God you got to her in time. How did you know where she was?"

"I got a text. I'm sure it was Julia who sent me the text. Enough about me. I can't believe you're pregnant. So I'll have two nieces or a niece and a nephew. Speaking of nieces, have you talked to Elie lately?"

"I tried calling her this morning to tell her about the baby. But she must have been busy. I'll call her tonight."

Just then Jonah walked. "Hey sweetheart, how's my little mommy?" Jonah said as he walked up to Rory and kissed her. And kissed her, and kissed her.

"You know when the baby's here, you'll have to do most of your kissing in the bedroom?" Kane said, grinning.

"Bull, our baby is going to know how much we love each other. I'll kiss my sweetheart as often as I can. Are you ready, sweetheart?"

"Yes, I want to finish the baby's bed and dressing I'm building. We won't paint it until we know what we are having. I'm so excited," Rory said, shedding a tear.

"I'm excited too, darling," he replied. Jonah wiped a tear from her cheek. "Are you going to cry the entire nine months?"

"Probably."

Kane thought his eyes might water, watching his sister. She was so happy. "I'm glad you got to come by and visit. Let me know if you talk to Elie."

"I will. I love you. When you have a few days off, come and stay with us. I miss you."

"I will. I'll call you as soon as I get some time off."

4

Kane called Austin. He was going crazy trying to answer these calls and tell which men to go where.

"Hey, buddy, how are you doing?"

"I'm going crazy. I can't figure out where everyone should go. Can you please come and show one of us how to do this paper crap."

"Kane, I have a cattle ranch to run. I don't have time to just stop in the middle of what I'm doing and come there because you need help. I figured it out. I'm sure you can too."

"Don't be a dick. I'm begging you. Please come show us how it's done."

"Okay, but you have to cook me a steak. I'll be there tomorrow. And you better take notes, because I don't have the time to go over it again with you. My ranch keeps me busy. And it is damn hard. I just bought some more horses, and there is a lot to do."

"Thank you! I'll see you in the morning."

Kane was pleased with himself. He ordered six steaks to be delivered. He had a massive grin on his face.

"Why are you so happy?" Ryes asked as he walked out to the backyard where Kane was standing.

"Austin is coming in the morning to tell us how he kept all the paperwork in perfect shape."

"Good. We need to hire someone full-time to take care of everything for us."

"I could do that."

Kane and Ryes turned around, and Riley stood there.

"I'm really good at that kind of stuff."

"What about school?"

"I can finish school on the computer. I only have two months left. Then I'm finished with college. This is just the kind of work I've been wanting to do. Something that keeps me busy and on my toes. You can give me a list of all the guys, and I'll get busy. I can install all the software on the computer. I feel so much stronger since coming here. I know it's only been two days, but I no longer feel sick, like I did before."

Kane looked at Riley. "You're hired. Austin will be here tomorrow. He can show you the ropes. Do you mind living here?"

"Not at all. I'm sure I'll love living here. I'm so happy. Thank you. I promise I will do a great job."

∼

"Hey Austin, how is ranch work treating you?" Kane said, pounding his friend on the back. He could swear someone else he knew had those same dimples when they smiled. He would give Elie a call.

"I like it. I miss everyone here, which surprises me. So tell me what's going on."

"We actually just hired an assistant to do the paperwork. She's here right now. Her name is Riley; she's one of our clients. She said she wants the job. Let's go find her."

"How is everyone?" Austin asked. He really wanted to know how Elie was doing, but he couldn't just come out and ask.

"I saw Jonah and Rory yesterday. They are having a baby."

"That's awesome. They will make great parents," Austin remarked. He stopped talking when Riley walked into the kitchen.

"Hello, you must be Riley," Austin said and stuck his hand out.

"Yes, and you must be Austin. I'm all ready for you to teach me what you know."

Austin smiled. His blond good looks and that sexy smile could melt the heart of any female, no matter her age. And Riley was no exception.

"Let's grab an ice tea to take along. Austin opened the fridge, and there was an entire pitcher of tea. "Thanks for making me tea," he said, looking at Kane.

"Hey, it's the least I could do since you've come all the way from Texas to help us out. So how is cattle ranching going?"

"It's hard work, but I enjoy it."

"Have you found yourself a Texan lady yet?"

"I'm not hunting for a lady," Austin replied, turning around. "Riley, if you will follow me to the office, I'll show you the ropes," he said and handed her a glass of the tea he poured.

"We also have some new recruits. Luke Wilson and Hunter Brown. Killian has managed to get a hold of a couple of others. I'm not sure how that worked out. Do you remember Luke and Hunter?"

"Of course, I do. Luke Wilson, I thought I recognized that Harley in the garage. I'm surprised he joined. I thought he was hitting the road on that bike of his since Susan died."

"He said after four years, he's ready to go back to work. He looks rougher than before. He was always laughing and having fun. But now he doesn't even crack a smile. His hair is too long and he needs to shave."

"He's hot," Riley said, taking a seat. "I think the sadness he's been through makes him more handsome, somehow," she remarked. Riley blushed when Austin and Kane smiled at her.

Austin chuckled. "You won't be the first young lady to fall for Luke."

"I'm not going to fall for him. You and Kane are just as handsome as Luke, but he has pain etched on his face. It makes most ladies want to help him. I'm not one of them. I have my own pain I have to deal with. So no men for me. If I was to fall for anyone, it would be Kane. He saved my life. I'll remember that for the rest of my life. I was about to be raped, and I thought I saw an angel standing behind the man I was trying to fight off, which wasn't much of a fight, and then Kane ripped him off of me and knocked him out cold. He's my hero. Plus, he's a great cook."

"I'm going to leave you two to the paperwork. Before I get a big head listening to Riley sing my praises. I have some calls to make," he said. Kane walked out and called his sister Elie. It went straight to her inbox. "Elspeth, I've been trying to get a hold of you for three days. If you don't call me back, I'm calling our cousins to go over there and see where the hell you are. How is baby Ivy doing? Send me some pictures of my beautiful niece. Bye, sweetie. Please call me."

His phone rang right away. "Kane, Ash needs you to pick him up. He's in Santa Monica. He's guarding a man who is in hiding. Can you go?"

"Yes, Austin is showing, Riley, our new assistant how to

do the paperwork. I'll have him stay here with her. Text me the address and anything else I need to know."

Kane stood in the doorway, watching Austin explain how things worked to Riley. "I have to run and pick Ash up. You are staying the night, right?"

"Yes, I'll stay the night. Riley and I will do just fine. I might even make us lunch. So go pick Ash up."

"I'll see you later."

Kane had been driving for about forty-five minutes when he noticed the exit. His phone rang then. "Hello."

"Where the fuck are you."

"I'm just down the street."

"Take the alley. Don't let anyone see you."

"I'm driving down the alley now. I see you. Why the hell are you running?" he asked. Kane looked in his rearview mirror and saw the vehicle coming up fast after them. "Fuck," he cursed. Kane reached over and flung open the door; Ash jumped in, and Kane hit the gas.

"Turn!" Ash shouted as another vehicle came straight at them. Bullets hit their car, and Kane felt one pierce his arm. He didn't have time to think about it. Three vehicles were chasing after them. The police showed up and took off after two of the cars. The other vehicle went down an alley. Kane pulled over when the police car pulled up behind them."

"Put your hands out the window," they ordered. The police opened their doors slowly they had their guns pointed at their heads. "Get out slowly. I want you down on the ground right now. I said get down!" the officer shouted.

"Look, I don't have time for this," Ash said to the officer. I have to save someone. We are the Band of Navy Seals high security team. Those men are after the man I'm guarding. I need to get to him before they find him," he explained. Ash looked over at Kane. "What the fuck. Were you shot?"

"It's only my arm. It'll be alright as soon as I can get off this damn filthy ground. Rocks are grinding into my face. Get my wallet out," Kane told the policeman. Another unmarked police car pulled up and stopped.

"Kane, Ash, what kind of trouble have you two gotten into now?"

"Hey, Paige, tell them who we are. Kane needs to go get his arm looked at, and I have to get to the man I'm guarding," Ash told his sister, who is a homicide detective.

"They're good guys," Paige told the police.

Kane looked over at Ash. "You can take my vehicle. Paige, can you give me a lift to the hospital?"

"Yes, hop in. How come those guys were after you?"

Kane got into the front seat. "Hell, if I know. I was supposed to pick your brother up, and the next thing I know, he's jumping into my vehicle, and someone is shooting at us."

"How's your arm?"

"It's not bad. I probably don't even need the doctor, but I know if I get an infection, then Frankie will be all over me."

Paige chuckled. "Yeah, I remember how angry she was that time Willow stepped on that nail, and her foot got infected. She gave her a long lecture. It's better if you get your arm checked out."

They both got out of the vehicle when they got to the hospital. "I'll go in with you in case they think you are running from the law or something."

"Okay, thanks"

"Hi, Kane, what happened? Did you get shot again?"

"Hi, Jill. Have you seen Frankie around?"

"I'm right here. Hi, Paige how are you doing?"

"I'm doing well. I just came to drop Kane off. He got shot in the arm."

"I see that. I was on my way to see Riley, so I can give you a ride home. How the heck did you get shot in the arm?"

"I went to pick up Ash. Some guys were shooting at us."

"Where is Ash?"

"He went to get his client."

"Who were these guys?"

"Hell if I know."

"You're lucky this is all that happened. It looks like you'll need some stitches, and I'll disinfect it."

"Yeah, I know how fortunate we are. I'm glad I got to Ash when I did. Hell, he was running down the alley as I pulled into it. They would have gunned him down. I don't know who he's guarding, but I guarantee you the guy didn't tell Ash everything, or there would have been more of us there guarding him."

"How does that feel?" Frankie asked after sewing Kane up.

"It feels good. Thanks."

"Well, I guess I'll be seeing you around. Tell Ash I'll be giving him a call. You can't be in a damn gunfight in the middle of the city," Paige said as she was leaving.

"Later," Kane said. He watched as Paige walked out of the emergency room. She reminded him of Emma Stone when she was a homicide detective. One bad-ass detective.

"Does she have a crush on you?"

"No, we went out a few times but realized we were better off just being friends."

"Do you want to tell me about Riley?"

"She's our new assistant. She is stunning, but she thinks she's ordinary. She has that special look. She said she had meningitis and hasn't recovered yet. She's twenty-two. Her Dad is DEA, and the cartels are after him. I barely got to Riley in time to save her from those men who were about to rape her. They had kidnapped her. She's lost a lot of weight, but she's been eating well since I brought her to the safe house. Her parents are at another safe house now. I think that's going to help her. She said they watched her every move."

"Yeah, I know people like that. They think their kids can't get by without them. The best thing is for them to move out."

"How are the babies doing?"

"They're wonderful. They bring so much joy to our lives. I'm no longer going to work unless it's an emergency."

"Really, do you think you will be able to stick to that?"

"Yes, I don't like leaving my babies even for an hour. They are so happy when they see me. I'm going to have another baby."

Kane looked at her and smiled, "Congratulations. I'm happy for you and Storm. I knew there was a reason that house you built was so big. Do you want to fill it with babies?"

"Yes, we do."

Kane laughed out loud. "Your kids are lucky to have you and Storm for parents. Rory and Jonah are having a baby too."

"That's wonderful. They must be so happy. Hey, you will be an uncle."

"Yeah, I'm already an Uncle."

"What? Are you saying Elie has a baby?"

"Yes, a beautiful baby girl with cute little dimples. Here look at her picture."

"She's beautiful. I wonder if we will have a girl. Is Elie with someone now?"

"No."

"Who is the daddy? I don't mean to be nosey. I'm sorry, it's none of my business."

"That's alright. I know nothing either. Austin is at the safe house teaching Riley about the handling of the paperwork. I haven't mentioned the baby to him. I figured if he cared for Elie, he would go get her."

"So Riley's going to work for you. Will Austin be here long enough to train her?"

"He came down this morning, and he's going to stay a couple of days, maybe longer."

"I thought for sure Austin and Elie would be together forever. They were always with each other. I don't mean just together like the rest of us at the hospital, waiting to see if Rory and Jonah would live. I mean together, together. If you know what I mean."

"I thought the same thing. I swear, even after the wedding, I felt for sure Elie would want to stay here."

"Maybe she was waiting for Austin to ask her to stay?"

"No, he was upset when she left. I think that's why he moved back to Texas."

"But he's had his ranch forever. We all knew he would go back there one day."

"He was going to stay until he turned forty. He's not forty. He still has a few years before he's forty."

"Hmm, how is Elie doing in Scotland?"

"She is doing great. I haven't spoken to her in a while. We haven't been able to get a hold of her. She's probably on a little vacation," he reasoned. Kane was still trying to figure out who Ivy's daddy was. He wasn't going to talk about something he knew nothing about. "Here we are."

Kane texted ahead to have Austin open the garage door. The garage opened, and Austin stood there grinning. "Why are you so happy?"

"That girl is brilliant. She's already redoing some things for the better. You'll have to pay her good money so she'll stay here. Hello sweet Frankie. You are more beautiful every time I see you. How is that husband of yours treating you? You are welcome to come home with me if he's mean to you."

"Austin, I'm having another baby. My husband treats me like I'm the best thing that has happened to him. I see you're as handsome as you've always been," she remarked. Austin laughed and pulled Frankie in for a hug.

"Congratulations on the little one. How are the boys doing?"

"Wonderful. I've missed you, Austin. Why did you stay away so long? You have to see the babies and Storm before you leave. Come out to the ranch. I know my brothers will want to see the guy who stayed on that horse longer than any of them could."

"Every time I'm ready to come here for a visit, one of the band shows up at my house. I can't leave them if they've come to visit me," he replied. Austin looked at Kane. "What happened to your arm, and where is your vehicle?"

"I was shot in the arm when I picked Ash up running down the alley. Ash has my vehicle because he had to track down his client. He'll be needing more men. I don't know who is after the client, but he lied when we took on the job. If Ash gets shot, someone will have to deal with Willow, and it won't be me."

"Damn, I'll call him and find out what the hell is going on. This will show Riley how sometimes someone throws a wrench in the spokes of our tires, and we do something else."

Kane chuckled. "You are starting to sound like an old man. Have you been hanging out with a bunch of old cowboys?"

Austin smiled and nodded. "Yes, crap, they are rubbing off on me," Austin joked. It felt good seeing his buddies. He actually missed them.

5

Julia had a stiff back from being in the same position for three hours. She didn't know she would get caught in someone's bedroom who was supposed to be at work. Julia sure as hell didn't know she would be listening to the woman having sex with one of the higher-up cartel men. She kept her fingers crossed that the lady's husband didn't show up and start shooting. She would have to hit the floor.

When she heard the shower going and both of them in it, she knew she had to get out of the closet. But she also knew there would be more of the cartel keeping watch, so she had to think. The only way she would get away without being caught was to sneak up to the attic. She would have to wait until they were all gone before she could leave. She was as quiet as a mouse going upstairs. But when she reached the top of the stairs, the attic door wouldn't open.

Julia never broke into a house without her tools. It took her ten seconds to open the locked door. The attic was hot and musky. She found a spot and made herself comfortable, thinking of Kane. That kiss almost had her dragging him to the bedroom. Kane was a great lover. The two of them would wake up three or four times a night and make love. She remembered how he would wake her and could feel herself getting hot. Too bad he had to fall in love with her.

She must have fallen asleep, as she heard shouting and jerked awake. There was fighting going on. Julia listened to the men fighting. Then came the gunfire. She pushed opened the door to see if she could hear anyone talking. All she heard was more shouting and gunfire. That went on for about ten minutes. Then it became quiet, and nothing. Julia walked down to the next floor. There was nothing but dead bodies. She counted seven of them. She took out her phone and reported it, then she left. Julia had no idea if anyone was still living. The ambulance would be there any minute. She went through the back door and over the fence. Most people put their cameras in the front and forgot about the back. She was almost over the wall when she heard something. She turned and saw the gun pointed at her. Julia didn't blink an eye before she had her gun out and fired. She shot him between the eyes then turned and jumped over the wall and ran to where she left her car. She turned the corner in time to see the police cars pulling into the driveway. "Call Skye," she said out loud.

"Hello."

"Skye, I was in Doreen's house when she and Pete Hugh came in. They started doing the f thing forever. I was hiding in the closet. I ended up in the attic when a gunfight started. I shot one man when I was climbing over the back wall. He spotted me and was going to shoot. You need to get the FBI there. There are dead people everywhere, I counted seven, but I didn't check to see if they were all dead. I'm guessing her husband and his men showed up."

"Damn it, Julia, I wish you would stop taking so many

damn chances with your life. Why were you in Doreen's house?"

"I wanted to see what I could find. I know it was Doreen who found out about Michelle being an agent. She turned her in, and they killed her. Now I think the bitch is dead, along with everyone that was there."

"Did you find anything?"

"No, because they showed up as I was looking."

"I'm going to go get this wig off and change my clothes, and then I'm going back as an FBI special agent. That way, I can start looking again."

"Are you trying to kill yourself? You be careful. I think you are taking too many chances with your life. You have three different disguises now. They're going to catch on. And I don't want to hear how good you are as an undercover agent. Are you trying to kill yourself? By the way, I have something important to tell you. And don't freak out. Kane was shot today."

"Wait? Kane who."

"Kane Walsh."

"My Kane was shot. I saw him yesterday. How the hell did he get shot?"

"He's alright. He was shot in the arm. His car was riddled with bullets."

Skye didn't know why Julia kept Kane at arm's length. She knew Julia cared for him. She told her she did. She was afraid if Kane loved her, he would die. Julia believed that people who loved her would die because of her parents dying, then her grandparents died, and she went into foster care. Until Skye adopted her. Julia must not think about Skye and her family, who love her. She probably blocks it from her mind.

"I've got to go," she said and hung up. *I can't believe Kane was shot. What the hell was he doing to have bullets flying into his vehicle?*

∽

JULIA STEPPED OVER THE BODIES. She stopped when she recognized a voice. She had plenty of time to hunt for the evidence she needed to see who turned Michelle over to the cartel. Julia was determined to avenge her death.

"What are you doing here?"

Hello, Paige. I'm looking into a shootout between two men who are supposed to be allies."

"Hmm, that's what I thought. Maybe they were after the same thing, and she's sitting over there," Paige said, she pointed by tossing her head. Doreen was sitting on a lounger by the window, looking frightened, which was all fake. "She said she saw a woman with blonde hair leaving the house. Do you know anything about that, Julia?" "

"HOW WOULD I know anything about that? I just got here. I'll go have a talk with Doreen."

"So, you know who she is?"

"Yes, she's married to that man by the bed, and she's that guy's mistress," Julia explained. Julia noticed Doreen putting a folded envelope in her bra. "I'll take that," Julia said, holding her hand out.

"I don't know what you're talking about."

"Come on, Doreen. We both know you put something in your bra. Either give it to me, or I'll take it."

Doreen looked up at Julia. "Who the fuck are you?"

"Special Agent Julia Sparrow FBI, at your service."

"Hmm, you remind me of someone. You can try to take it from me, but I assure you, I'll scream rape. I don't care if you are a woman," Doreen replied. Julia saw her squint her eyes and look at her again.

Julia snickered. "Your husband and your lover are both dead. You don't seem to be at all upset about it."

"He was not my lover. He murdered my husband. How dare you talk to me this way? I'll make sure you lose your job over this."

"How will you do that? Do you think your other lover, our district attorney, will have the authority to fire me?" she asked. Julia kept an eye on Doreen and realized that scared her.

"I don't know what you're talking about."

"Sure you do. Now give me the envelope," Julia ordered. Before Doreen realised what had happened, Julia reached in and took the envelope from down the front of her blouse. "Sit your ass down," Julia said as Doreen jumped up. "Arrest this woman, and make sure you read her rights to her," Julia told a police officer who walked into the room.

"That is private property. Give me back my mail."

Julia took the envelope over to where Paige stood, writing things down on a piece of paper. "Look at this. Doreen was also sleeping with the district attorney. He is the one who gave her the information about Michelle, so he must be getting money from the cartel. So we need to have someone go arrest him before he has a chance to run."

"Wow, I wonder who else she's slept with?" she wondered. Paige looked at Julia. "Fuck, you forgot to take your contacts out."

Julia turned towards the wall and took them out. It was that damn news about Kane being shot. It was making her careless. She had to be more careful. She was angry. Michelle was her friend. The way she was murdered haunted her every night. "I'm going to go through every inch of this place.

Hell, if the district attorney knew about a certain lady agent, he would have turned her over to the cartel as well."

"I'll help you. It won't do any good to arrest her. She'll be out in two hours."

"What else can I do with her?"

"Let the cartel have her. They'll take care of her. Look at the mess she's caused."

"That will still give us two hours to go through this house."

"That's true."

They watched as the police walked her out of the room. Julia and Paige went over every inch of the space but found nothing in the bedroom. They searched the rest of the house but still found nothing.

Paige looked at Julia. "I guess they held her."

"Something isn't right," Julia said. "Why would District Attorney Desantis keep her? You know she had to tell him I have the letter. Unless he's already flown the coop."

Paige took out her phone and called the precinct. "This is Lieutenant Paige Beckham. Has Doreen Kant's been charged with anything yet?"

"Let me check," the officer said. It was on loudspeaker, so they both could hear. "There isn't a Doreen Kants who was brought in here. I checked the other precincts as well. No one with that name has been brought into any of the other precincts."

"Fuck, it was either the district attorney or the cartel, but one of them took Doreen, and I bet you she's dead," Julia said, shaking her head. "I'll get my wig back on and go see the boss."

"You need to be careful. I think something big is about to happen. I've been hearing some talk on the street. They say most of the dealers are laying low."

. . .

"Believe me, I know that. That's why I've been staying so close to Juan. As much as I hate him, I know I have to be near him. You know the saying, 'keep your enemies close.' That's what I've been doing. Now I have to go see what's going on with Jaun's end of the cartel.

6

Kane looked at his clock. It was three in the morning. He should try and go back to sleep. This is the third time he's woken up. He decided to get up and make a cup of coffee. He threw on some sweats. As he walked barefoot into the kitchen, he heard someone singing. He smiled as he stopped and listened to Riley singing. She did her best, and he smiled as she tried hitting a note.

"Yay!! Encore."

Riley laughed. "Oh, no, I already know I sound like a cat screaming. My dad has told me many times. I can't sing. But I enjoy it so much, I sing anyway."

"Good for you. Why are you up?"

"I decided to make dinner tonight, and I wanted to make sure we have everything. Plus, I couldn't go back to sleep. Does your arm hurt?"

"It's a bit stiff. I need coffee. Would you like a cup?"

"I would love a cup of coffee. I started drinking coffee when I was twelve. I've always been an early riser. I started making coffee way back then. I'm actually a shareholder in a coffee company. My friends started when we were in high school."

"So, does that mean we get free coffee from now on?"

"Yes, you also get free hot chocolate. I'm so happy I have this job. You don't even know. I'll make breakfast this morning. I'm actually a good cook. It's one of my favorite things to do."

"Oh yeah, that's great. I cook most meals here because the others try to out wait me, and they usually win. I have to have my food, or I get grumpy. I don't mind cooking, so we can take turns."

"Okay, I'm going to get dressed."

That's when Kane noticed she was in her jammies. He looked down, and he didn't have a shirt on. He'd have to remember to dress before coming out of his room. "Yeah, me too," he said and ran upstairs to change his clothes.

They sat at the table drinking a cup of coffee when Austin walked in the kitchen for a cup of coffee in his boxers. Kane looked at Riley, and both of them laughed. Kane thought it was going to be nice having a woman around the house, especially one who had a sense of humor.

"What?" Austin said.

"We have a lady in the house, and you're pouring a cup of coffee in your boxers."

Austin looked down and grinned. "I'll take my coffee to my room and get dressed."

"Thank you, Austin. I am a bit shy. I've never seen a man in his boxers before."

Kane's phone rang. "Hello,"

"How's your arm?"

"It's okay, you know me, and my skin is tough as old hide. How did you hear about it?" he asked. Kane walked out of the kitchen. He needed to hear her voice. He always thought her voice sounded like a warm cup of malt whiskey. It made him hot every time she talked to him.

"Skye told me."

"Skye, how the hell did she know?"

"I don't know. What are you doing?"

"Having coffee. I miss you. Can we please talk?"

"Kane, I miss you too. I want to talk to you. I'm going to be out of town for a few days. When I get back, we'll talk."

Kane was in his room by now. He leaned against the wall and closed his eyes. "Call me the minute you get home."

"I will, I promise. Bye, Kane."

"Bye, Julia."

He sat on his bed and held his head in his hands. "Thank you for helping to send Julia back to me," he whispered.

"Kane, are you in here?" Austin said, knocking on his door.

"Yeah, I'm here," he said, standing up and opening the door. "What's up?"

"I've had a call from Luke. He said they need another man. Who is available?"

"Hell, let me see."

Riley joined in the discussion. "Arrow is available. I've already called him. He wants to talk to one of you because he doesn't know who I am," Riley said. She smiled then giggled. "He said he was supposed to go surfing with Austin tomorrow."

"Damn, I forgot all about that," Austin said, walking out of the room. "I'll explain to everyone who you are and tell him we'll go surfing when the job is over. I'll also call the DEA and have them put your parents in the witness protection program," Austin said. He looked at Riley. "Will that bother you? You might only see your parents once yearly or twice a year."

"I'll miss them, but we do what we have to do. I'm going

to be here. Getting healthy, and they will be somewhere safe with a new identity. I finally feel safe, and I like the feeling."

"Good, let's go talk to Arrow. Then we'll call Lucas and tell him to get on it. They should have already been on this. One other thing, don't hesitate to go after the people who need to get it together and do their job."

"Okay. Are you sure you can't stay longer? I need to learn how you tell the people what they need to do."

"I'll call my ranch and tell them I'm staying a week. I'll hang out here with you. You will be the best assistant anyone has ever had. You ever been surfing?"

"Thank you for staying longer, and no, I've never surfed. Maybe when I get healthy, I can give it a try."

"Have you been ill a long time?"

"It seems like forever. It's been over a year. But since being here, I can feel myself getting stronger. I kind of feel like I'm free. Isn't that silly?"

"No, that's not silly. Your body knows how it feels."

"Do you surf a lot?"

"I like to compete in surfing competitions."

∽

"Dinner was delicious," Austin remarked. He looked at Riley. "I feel like I'm at an expensive restaurant. Did you take cooking lessons?"

"No, my mom taught me how to cook. She was a famous chef in New York before she married my dad. After she became pregnant with me, she quit working. I always wondered if she ever regretted getting married and throwing away her career. I guess she did what she wanted to do. Before I came along, she was recognized everywhere, and then they moved to California, and she became known as Jerry's wife."

"Why did she quit working?"

"I think my dad must have talked her into staying home with me. He didn't trust anyone to watch me. I think it has something to do with him being a DEA officer."

Austin took another bite of his food. "Women need their own life outside of being married. My mom was a high school teacher until she retired last year. Now she enjoys staying with her grandkids. They're great kids. I've kept them overnight a few times. The youngest is three. She's a beauty and as sassy as they come. She always has to climb in bed with me. Before the morning comes along, they are all in my bed. Wait until you are an uncle Kane, you'll have them staying with you."

"That'll be fun," he remarked. Kane got up and started doing the dishes. He didn't mention he had a niece who was beautiful with cute dimples. He wanted to talk to Austin about Elie, but he couldn't. It wasn't his story to tell. "I'm going to hit the hay early tonight. Frankie will be here early. She's bringing the boys with her. I'm going to need all the rest I can get to run after two toddlers."

"Me too," Riley said, yawning.

Austin decided to make himself a cup of coffee. "I'm going to have a cup of coffee. I'll see you two tomorrow."

"You're having coffee at night. It doesn't keep you awake?"

"No. That's an old wives tale. I have a cup every night. I think it helps me to sleep."

Kane laughed. "Austin loves his coffee more than anyone I know. Good night."

7

It had already been four days, and Julia hadn't called. Kane decided if she didn't call tomorrow, he would call Skye. If Julia said she would call in a few days, then that's what she would do. One thing about Julia was that she did exactly what she said she would do. He threw the pillow across the room and got up, another sleepless night. He took a shower and got dressed. He then made some coffee and walked out the back door. There was a light on in the house behind their house. It was one of their safe houses, but no one was supposed to be there. Kane pulled his gun out and opened the gate with the hidden button. When he slipped into the backyard, Ash was back there talking on the phone. He waved to Kane. Kane sat in the chair next to him with his coffee.

"My wife misses me, and I miss her. This guy has lied too many times. I don't know who he's running from, but I called Lucas and asked him to see what he could find out. I don't want him to know about the house you're in. I don't know enough about him. I'm thinking of handing him over to someone else if he doesn't start telling the truth."

"I wonder what he's up to. Did you find out who was shooting at us?"

"He's made someone very angry, and I don't know anything else. He's very wealthy. I've tried finding him online, but he's not even on the damn internet."

"I can ask Riley to see what she can find; she's a whiz on the computer. You'll really like Riley a lot. She has shares in a coffee company, so we are all set up. She even had some coffee stuff shipped to Austin's ranch."

"I'm damn glad we have an assistant to take care of everything. I won't have to try and figure out how to organize everyone. Have you seen Luke or Hunter?"

"Yes, Luke has a tortured look about him. I think he took this job in the hope of being shot. Hunter is the same as always, easy-going. He goes with the flow. I better get back to my own yard before your client wakes up."

"Wakes up, hell he won't wake up, that guy sleeps until late in the afternoon. He plays games on the computer all night with his buddies."

"Hopefully, he doesn't tell them where he is. No telling who is playing those games…" Kane stopped talking and looked at Ash, who was smiling.

"It's his so-called buddies. He must play with some heavy hitters. Like maybe some mafia dudes, who he owes a lot of money."

"That's it. He's a gambler, who plays with money he doesn't have until a particular time of the month. He must get money at a specific time of the month. Like maybe his grandma gives him an allowance. Well, you know what you have to do. Talk to him about his gambling and ask him if he really wants to pay for a high-security firm to guard him all the time," Kane reasoned. He then got up and walked through the gate and back inside the house.

~

THEY HAD JUST SAT down to dinner when Skye came in. The look on her face scared the hell out of Kane. He jumped up and went to her. "Where is she?"

"We don't know. Julia said they dumped her body, thinking she was dead. She could barely talk. Her voice was so week I barely heard her."

Skye looked at Lucas, and he finished telling Kane what happened. "She said she was beaten for two days. She was tricked. When she went to see Juan, Doreen was there. She's one of the wives involved in a big shooting last week between her husband and his men, as well as her lover and his men. She recognized Julia from when she went to her house as herself, an FBI agent. Apparently Doreen had escaped police custody. Because when Julia called to see where Doreen was she hadn't even been brought in to be booked.

"Julia didn't know where she was because they threw her body out of the moving vehicle. Those fuckers thought she was dead. She said she didn't think she had much time left. Julia said she was dying. And then her phone went dead. What are we going to do?"

"We're going after her. Doreen will wish she was never born, and so will Juan. Did you bring everything with you?" The veins in Kane's neck were standing out. He was so angry he wanted to yell out loud.

"Yes. I'll get dressed. Is there anyone else available?"

"Luke and Hunter will be here any minute. Riley's parents went into a witness protection program. Until they arrest the people after them, it'll be a few years before they're out of hiding.

Austin stood up. "I'll get dressed. I'm going with you."

Kane looked at Riley. "Do you think you'll be alright by yourself?"

"Yes, I'll be fine. Don't worry about me. I have a gun. If I need to use it, I will. My dad taught me how to shoot guns years ago."

"Okay, I'll have Ash keep an eye out. He's in the house behind us. That also is a safe house."

"Okay, don't worry about me. Go find Julia."

8

All of them had on black tactical gear, and their weapons strapped to them. Riley counted five knives and three guns on Skye. When Luke and Hunter walked in, Kane explained what was going on. They changed their clothes and joined them. There were six of them in total and they were headed to Jaun's home.

Being Navy Seals, they could slip in and out of places without being seen. All of them rubbed some kind of mask on their face and put on their black beenies. Kane went over the wall first. He was on his stomach looking around. He tapped his watch, and Luke was beside him. Luke moved his head, and Kane saw three guards who walked the perimeter of the wall. He wondered if any of them were in on the beating of Julia. Kane didn't have a lot of time. He nodded once, and Luke leaped at the men at the same time as him. The men were down, and they didn't even know what hit them.

He looked at the wall. The others were over it, standing against it. They communicated only through hand signals and never spoke. Lucas spotted the cameras, and Kane pulled something out of one of his pockets. He swung it upwards, the wire wrapped around the camera, and brought it down. Kane had brought down three more before someone came to check on them. Two men who were so loud anyone could hear them. They weren't too bright the way they were shouting and laughing. Kane heard them talking about Julia. "Whoever she was, Doreen didn't like her," one man said, "I wish she would have killed Doreen. I hate that bitch. My brother was in that shoot-out she caused. It was all planned. She and the district attorney planned it," the bastard laughed, "I bet that district attorney was surprised when she shot him in the head."

"Yeah, I really didn't like killing the other woman. She could fight better than any of Juan's men. She was one hot babe too. We should have gotten us some of that before we killed her and dumped her body. Hell, it took six of us to take her down."

Kane had him around the throat. Skye had already killed the other guy. That's why Kane grabbed this one before she killed him. He was going to show them where Julia was. Or he would start cutting his fingers off and then his dick. He slammed his fist in the man's face, but he made sure he didn't blackout. You're going to show us where you dumped the lady. If you do it right, I'll let you live. If not, I'm going to start cutting things off. Remember that whatever dangles will be cut off if you don't do as we say."

"Kill me. Juan will kill me anyway."

"He won't be able to kill you if he's dead," he replied. Kane looked up as Luke, Lucas, and Skye walked to where they were. "Are they dead?"

"Those bastards took their last breath," Skye said and hit the guy in the throat.

"I'm not going to let you kill him. I told him I would let him live if he takes us to where he pushed Julia out of the vehicle," he told her. Kane dragged him to their vehicle and threw him inside. "Start talking."

"Go south on Carpenter road, all the way up into the woods. About three miles up is where we dropped her out of the vehicle."

"You mean you threw her out of the vehicle when you were driving. You bastard!" Skye shouted.

Kane knew Skye was going to kill the guy. He looked at her and saw it in her eyes.

"Right here. Stop here."

They stopped the car, and Kane jumped out, shouting Julia's name. "Julia, where are you! Please, God, let us find her," Kane pleaded. He walked down about ten feet and walked along the road. All he could hear was Skye, screaming and crying, afraid of what she would find. "Skye, please be quiet. I can't hear anything. Julia, sweetheart, say something. Please say something," he called out. They were there for thirty minutes before Kane found anything. His foot hit something, Kane bent down to pick it up. *It's her phone; thank goodness for the headlights.* Thirty minutes later, he found her. His heart was in his stomach. His hand gently touched her face. "I found her!" he shouted. Skye called for an ambulance then.

He held her limp body in his arms, trying to see where she was injured. Her hair was matted with her blood. Skye was next to him on her knees. Kane felt everywhere on her for a bullet or a knife wound. Luke brought their vehicle closer, so the headlights were shining right on her. Skye had stopped crying, and now she was checking all over Julia's body. Kane took her jacket off and raised her T-shirt up. All he could see were bruises. She had cuts on her side. Her arm was really damaged. It looked to be broken in a few spots.

Her foot or ankle was also broken. Bruises were everywhere. They covered her entire body. It seemed like they hit her with something, maybe a belt buckle.

"This head wound is causing some damage," Skye said.

"What are you talking about?"

"The back of her head is cracked, and it's going to need to be sewed. She has so much dirt caked in her hair I'm having a hard time seeing anything. That might have happened when they threw her from the vehicle. She has a slight pulse. She's not dead like she thought she was going to be. Here's the ambulance. I'll ride with her. Where is the man?"

"He must have taken off," Lucas said. As soon as the words left Lucas's mouth, he knew he shouldn't have told them. Skye jumped up.

"Skye," Lucas said, "let's worry about Julia right now and forget that man. He'll die anyway, once he gets back to where we took him from."

Skye nodded and stood back when the ambulance men walked over. Lucas explained who they were, and they loaded Julia and Skye into the ambulance. When the police drove up, Luke and Hunter walked over to them.

"Someone will have to come to the precinct and leave a statement," the officer said.

"We'll drop you and Lucas off at the hospital," Austin said, "then we'll swing by and leave a statement."

Kane kept his head down. He didn't want the guys to see the tears in his eyes. "That would be great, Austin."

Austin put his hand on Kane's shoulder and squeezed. "Kane, you have to think positive. Julia is as tough as any of us. She's going to pull through this. You'll see. Everything will be fine."

Kane didn't say anything. He nodded his head. All he could see was Julia's lifeless body in his arms.

"Kane, let's trade places."

He heard someone calling his name, and he raised his head. It was Skye. "What?"

"You go with Julia. I'll ride with Lucas."

Kane jumped out of the vehicle and jumped into the back of the ambulance. He took Julia's hand and brought it to his mouth. He watched as the EMTs worked on her. They talked to a doctor at the hospital the entire time. They hooked her up with an IV and oxygen. They cut her jeans all the way up to her thighs. And cut open her shirt.

"Fuck, who would do this to her? He must have been a sick bastard."

"Six men beat Julia. They've all paid for what they've done," Kane said.

The EMT was talking to the doctor at the hospital. "She has broken bones in her left arm. Her right ankle is broken in at least three places. Her head injury seems to have caused a substantial amount of damage," the EMT reported. He shook his head as he gently turned Julia. "Those bastards really did some damage. She has a few deep cuts," the man said. He continued to talk to the doctor, telling the doctor everything he could. "She has an injury to her head. She was thrown from a moving vehicle, so that may have happened when she hit the ground."

When they pulled into the emergency entrance, Luke pulled in behind them. There was a doctor and two nurses who took over. They transferred Julia to another bed and pushed her through the doors. One of the nurses turned to Skye and Kane. "You'll have to wait in the waiting room."

Skye ignored her, as did Kane.

Lucas put his arm around Skye. "Skye, let's let the doctors help her. They'll let you know as soon as they find out what is going on with Julia."

"Get me an orthopedic surgeon," the doctor yelled while

pushing Julia. He stopped and looked at them. "I'm going to do everything I can to help her. I'll come and talk to you the first chance I get."

They nodded and walked out to the waiting room.

9

Kane paced the hallways of the hospital. He couldn't sit in that room waiting for news of Julia's condition. He had to do something. He turned the corner, and Luke stood talking to a nurse. It seemed like he might have known the nurse.

"I'll see you around. Here's my buddy. I was looking for you. The doctor is going to come and talk to everyone. Did you turn your phone off?"

"Yeah, sorry about that. Did you know that nurse?"

"Yeah, we've gone out a few times." They were walking back to the waiting room, "Sometimes I can't look at myself in the mirror. I sleep with women and the entire time I can't stop thinking about my wife. Susan has been gone for four years. She was my life. You have to take life by the horns and convince Julia that the two of you belong together. Don't let a minute go by without telling her how much you love her. You don't want to end up like me and be miserable for the rest of your life."

They saw Skye looking out of the doorway. "There you

are? Your phone must have died. The doctor is coming to talk to us. Thanks, Luke, for finding him."

When the doctor stepped into the waiting area, Kane didn't know he was holding his breath until he let it out. "Julia is in pretty good shape for the beating she took. Her arm and her ankle are broken. Her arm will take quite a while to heal. Her ankle won't take as long. She's in surgery right now. The doctor is putting the bone in her arm together. Her head injury is not life-threatening. We are going to sew it up, but we want to make sure there is no swelling."

"As you know, she has multiple more injuries to her body that will all take some time to heal. The main thing is she'll live. Julia's going to be in a lot of pain. You just have to let her know you are there for her, even if she is grumpy. Now I need to tell the nurses in ICU what they'll need to do when Julia get's there."

"Thank you for taking the time to talk to us," Kane said, shaking his hand. He looked at his buddies. "You all should go home. I'll get a ride back to the house."

"Call if you need anything."

"I will," Kane replied. He looked at Skye and Lucas. "Why don't I go get us a cup of coffee?"

"I would like that," Skye said.

"Me too," Lucas agreed.

They were drinking their coffee when the nurse came in looking for them. Kane felt his heart fall to the pit of his stomach. It couldn't be good news the doctor had just talked to them. "What's wrong?"

"Julia had a seizure while they were doing surgery. She's going to be alright. They have to wait before they can finish the surgery. Julia is going for some cat scans. The doctor wants to make sure everything is okay before he continues.

We just wanted to let you know it'll be longer than we thought before you can see Julia."

"She must have some pressure on her brain that caused the seizure. They can let the pressure off, right?" Kane said, looking at the nurse.

"Yes, if it is caused by pressure on her brain, the doctor will have to take care of that first. We will keep you informed. Could I get one of your phone numbers? That way, we'll just call you and not have to hunt for you."

Kane gave her his phone number, and Skye gave her phone number too.

Skye looked at Lucas. "Why don't you go home with the children. I'll call you when I hear something."

"Are you going to be okay?"

"Yes, I promise. I know Julia's going to live. That's what matters. Whatever else there is, we'll deal with it when it happens," he said. Lucas pulled Skye into his arms and kissed her. "Call me if you need me. I love you, sweetheart."

"I love you too."

Kane called Rory and explained what was going on.

"Oh my God, that's horrible. I'll come and sit with you."

"No, there isn't anything you can do. I would rather brood on my own. I'll call you as soon as we hear something."

"Okay, if you change your mind, call me. I love you."

"I know. I love you too. Did I tell you Austin is here to train our new assistant? I know where wee Ivy gets her dimples from."

"I thought the same thing. I was going to say something to you. When I saw Ivy's dimples, all I could see was Austin smiling. What are we going to do about it? He deserves to know he has a beautiful baby girl."

"After this emergency with Julia is over, we'll do something. Until then, I don't think I can handle another crisis."

"I agree. I haven't talked to Elie in over a week. She must

be swamped. I've left her like three messages."

"Yeah, me too. Hopefully, everything is okay," he said. Kane shook his head. "I'm sure everything is fine. You take care of yourself, Rory. I'll call you later."

"Okay, bye. I'll talk to you later."

Kane hung up the phone and thought of Elspeth. *What is going on with her? Why doesn't she answer her damn phone?* He walked back to the waiting room and watched Skye. Kane smiled. He was glad Skye adopted Julia, no telling what kind of life she would have had. "Let's go to the café and get something to eat. They have our phone numbers so if they need us, they'll call.

"You're right. I could use a glass of tea and a sandwich. Stuff like this puts a lot of stress on your body. I bet you feel like you live at this hospital. You've been here so often this last year. How is your family doing? I see Rory once in a while, but what about your other sister Elspeth. Does she get lonely in Scotland by herself?"

"We have lots of cousins who live in Scotland. One of them is usually at the farm. Rory and I miss her. I have actually called her a few times and haven't gotten ahold of her. She's swamped this time of year with sheering the sheep."

"I'm fortunate I had Sage claim me as a sister when we were all in foster care. That gave us all the chance to have a family."

"That's right, Arrow has told me about how you became a family. It was remarkable that kids knew they wanted to be a family and stuck to it as any typical family. When you are all together, you can tell you were raised together and love each other. I think that is great."

It's all because of Sage. She wouldn't leave us alone. She was determined we were going to be a family. I'm glad we decided to eat together. I know you and Julia love each other. Julia is afraid for someone to love her. I shouldn't be telling you this. So don't say anything to Julia. She thinks if someone loves her, they'll die. Her family all died, and she thought it was because she loved them. She is obsessed with this. She knows we all love her, but we can't tell her out loud. Or we will die. I know it sounds crazy, but that's been in her head since she was a child."

"When you told Julia you loved her, it scared the hell out of her. She was convinced you were going to die. No matter how much I told her you wouldn't. I couldn't convince her that it was crazy thinking. So she thought she would make you not love her by staying away from you."

"That could never happen. I love Julia too much to ever stop loving her."

"I know that, and I think Julia knew it too. I was surprised when she showed up at the hospital when Rory was in there. She wanted to give you comfort because she loves you," she told him. Skye looked into his eyes. She has to quit working. Too many bad people know her. I have to convince her to move away. I'm sure everyone on the streets has heard by now that she's an undercover FBI special agent. I need you to help me convince her to quit her job."

"I'll do everything I can to convince her. I hate that damn job she has. Why she decided to do undercover jobs is beyond me. You can count on me. But we won't say anything about it until she's healed. There is nothing worse than trying to get someone to do something they don't want to do."

"I agree. Whew, I'm happy I have you helping me with this."

"We both love Julia and only want the best for her."

"Yep," Skye said as she finished drinking her tea.

10

Kane heard her before he reached her room. She and Skye were having a loud discussion. He knew what it was about. Skye wanted Julia to move back in with them, and Julia said she would never put them in a position where Skye and Lucas had to take care of her. Kane walked into the room smiling. He had the perfect solution. He knew it would take some convincing on his part. Hopefully, Julia would listen to him. They'd been arguing about this for the last two weeks. Julia tried her best to keep Kane away. He ignored her just like Skye did.

"Why are you smiling? While I'm at it, why do you come here every day to see me? Don't you listen to anything I say? God, it's like talking to a wall," Julia ranted. *I can't believe he still comes here. I'm not going to tell him how much I love him. If I tell Kane I love him, he'll die. I can never tell him. Every time I tell someone I love them, they die. I can't risk something happening to Kane. I know that is stupid. I wish I didn't feel this way.*

Kane shrugged his shoulders. "The woman I love is alive and very vocal. What's not to smile about?"

Julia shook her head. *What am I suppose to say to that?*

"Skye, I'm not moving in with you. You have your own family to take care of."

"You are my family. You are my first child. It doesn't matter a damn that I was twenty-three, and you were fifteen when I adopted you. So that makes you as close to me as my children. Stop arguing with me over this. I have to go. I'll be back before tonight."

"You don't have to come every day. You have a family to take care of and a job."

"Goodbye, Julia," she said. Skye looked at Kane and smiled. "Hello and goodbye Kane, maybe you can talk some sense into Julia. I sure can't."

Kane smiled at Skye as she left. "I'll see you later, Skye."

Julia looked at him. "Why are you still smiling? And why do you always take her side? You know how stubborn she is."

"I didn't say I was taking her side. You can't go home on your own. Your arm is broken in numerous places, and your ankle is broken. You have other injuries that haven't had time to heal. You have to stay with someone," Kane said. He looked like the cat who got the cream. "I have the perfect solution."

"What is this perfect solution?" Julia asked, trying unsuccessfully to get comfortable.

"Marry me, Julia. I love you, and you know you love me. I know I'm not supposed to say that out loud, but I'm going to keep saying it. Skye will stop worrying about you, and you will make me the happiest man alive."

"Are you crazy? I'm not going to have you take care of me. Jeez, Kane, what have you been smoking?"

"Answer me this, do you love me?"

"I'm not going to answer that," Julia said, stubbornly turning her head so Kane couldn't see the sadness in her eyes.

Kane sat on the bed and gently pulled her onto his lap.

Her hospital gown was slipping off of her, and he fixed it. He somehow made her comfortable. She shouldn't love him so much. She relaxed and rested her head on his shoulder. It felt so lovely for Kane to hold her again.

"Julia, I love you. I've been in love with you for three years. Don't you think it's time you tell me how much you love me?"

"Kane," she began. Julia was so afraid to love Kane as much as she did. It was bad luck for people to love her. She knew that was stupid, but she couldn't help it. That's been her biggest fear. *God, can I let Kane love me? I guess he's loved me all this time, and nothing has happened. Can I tell him? Can I marry him and have children? My own children. This world is such a scary place to raise kids. I know that more than most. I've rescued so many girls and boys from the cartel who were involved in human trafficking. Even people in our own government are involved in the selling of women and children.*

"What do you say, Julia, will you marry me?"

Tears fell from her eyes. She loved him. "I love you so much it scares me," Julia replied. This was the first time she ever said she loved him out loud.

Kane shook on the inside. This was the first time Julia had ever told him she loved him. "Sweetheart, there is nothing to be afraid of. I love you. Will you be my wife?"

"Dare I take the chance? I'm scared to love you," Julia admitted. She looked into his eyes. "Yes, I'll be your wife. I hope you don't regret asking me."

Kane laughed out loud and kissed her. He looked at how beautiful she was inside and out. "I'll never regret asking you to marry me," Kane told her. He looked into her eyes, bent his head, and kissed her again.

"Kane, I've missed your kisses. I'm so happy everything is out in the open. And I can tell you I love you. When should we get married?" Julia asked. "You have to make Skye understand I am not moving in with her family."

"We'll get married today. We'll have the hospital chaplain marry us as he did for Jonah and Rory. And, of course, you aren't moving in with them. You will be my wife, and you will live with me."

Julia frowned. "We don't have rings. I don't want you taking care of me either."

Kane ignored what she said about him not taking care of her. She was going to be his wife. It was his responsibility to take care of her. "Yes, we do have rings. Kane put his hand in his pocket and pulled out an old-looking small box. I've carried these rings with me for years. In a small village near our home in Scotland, a ring maker makes unique rings for people. When I was fifteen, the 'ring maker,' that's what everyone called him, called out to me when I was walking past his shop. He took me into his store and said, 'I made you and your bride's wedding rings for you.' I told him I was only fifteen, and I wasn't getting married. He told me the fairies don't care how old you are. Then he showed me these rings.

Kane opened the box and showed Julia.

Julia held her breath when Kane opened the box; she thought she might cry. "They are gorgeous," she whispered, "did he let you have them then and there?"

"No, I worked for him for six months, then he gave me the rings. I would have worked for him longer than that, but he said they were paid off. I knew the fairies made these rings for my bride and me. I was fifteen and secretly believed in fairies."

Julia wiped away a tear. "I'm sorry for being afraid of letting you love me. Only you have to promise to please always be careful. It would kill me if something happened to you. I wanted to tell you I loved you. But then I remembered telling my mom and dad I loved them, and they died that same day. When my grandparents took me in, they were grief-stricken. I told them I loved them so they wouldn't be so sad. They both died when a crazy man went to McDonald's and started shooting. I was at school when the police came and told me what happened. I was ten years old. I never tell Skye and Lucas I love them. I don't even tell the babies how much I love them. I know that's silly. I'm going to change, I promise. Just stay safe, okay."

"I promise, sweetheart, nothing will happen to me because we love each other."

"I'm telling you, this frigging sucks. I don't like being helpless. You have to get me a nurse. I don't want you doing everything for me. I need to learn to manage on my own. Until I get these casts off. I swear I thought I would be dead before you found me. All I could think of was I wish I would have told you how much I loved you, and I never told you," Julia revealed. She looked into his eyes and smiled, "I can't always count on you doing everything for me," she said. Julia took a deep breath. "Damn, this sucks."

"What sucks, marrying me?"

Julia smiled. "No, you're the only man I have ever loved. I don't like the idea of marrying you while I'm in this shape."

"I'd marry you no matter what shape you were in," he replied. Kane pushed the nurse button.

The nurse smiled when she saw Julia sitting on Kane's lap. "What can I do for you?"

"Julia and I are getting married. Can you please tell me how I can get ahold of the chaplain?"

"I'll call him right now. I'm so excited for you both. I know how much you love each other."

Kane looked at Julia. "I have loved Julia forever."

Julia ducked her head under Kane's chin and cuddled closer. "I'm so lucky Kane loves me. And he wouldn't give up on me," she remarked. Julia smoothed her hair back and remembered the nurse shaved some of it when they had let the pressure off her brain. *I can't get married without something covering my head.*

"What is it, sweetheart?"

"I need something to cover my head. I can't get married to the man I love with most of my hair shaved off."

Kane looked at the door as Missy walked in.

"Hello, you two. You look like you're having a serious conversation."

Julia smiled. Missy was her best friend. From the moment they met, Missy declared they would be best friends forever. "Missy, Kane and I are getting married."

"That's wonderful. I'm so happy for you two. When is the big day?"

"Today. You can be our witness. But what am I going to do about my hair?"

"I'll fix your hair. All I'll need is a pair of scissors. I'm so excited. Are your family members on their way?"

"No, we haven't told anyone except you. Are you sure you can fix my hair?"

"Yes, I'll go get some scissors from the nurse's station. I'll be right back."

Julia cuddled up to Kane as good as she could with a broken ankle and a broken arm with a cast that wouldn't move. "Thank you, Kane, for not giving up on us."

"I could never give up on us, sweetheart. You know you can ask me anything, and I'll do it."

"I know. It worries me that my body is so messed up right now. I'm used to being healthy. I want us to be equal partners in our marriage. But I feel like you'll be the only one giving."

"No, that's not true. You've given me so much by agreeing to marry me. I love you, and you love me. That's all that matters. You'll be your old self soon. Don't worry about that now."

"Okay, let me tackle this hair," Missy said, walking back into the room. she looked at Kane and Julia. "You'll have to unwrap yourself from Kane's body, or I might accidentally poke Kane," Missy said, picking up strands of Julia's hair and started cutting.

"Have you ever cut anyone's hair, Missy?" Julia asked.

"Nope, but you know me, I like trying all sorts of things out. It's already looking so much better," Missy looked at Julia and busted out laughing, "you should see your face. I wish I would have had my camera out. Yes, I've cut hair before. I've been cutting my own hair since I was fifteen. And I have to say I give Polly better haircuts than her salon lady."

"Is there anything you haven't done?"

"Yes, there are tons of things. I haven't ever fallen in love. I haven't flown a plane on my own yet. I haven't climbed Mt. Everest. I haven't had children. There are loads of things I haven't done. There, I'm finished. I have to say you are one beautiful lady."

"Thank you."

"I'll help you to the mirror," Kane said as he picked her up.

"Wow, I have wavy bouncy hair. I love it. Thank you, Missy. I might keep it this short; it feels so nice and light."

"You're welcome. Here put this sweater on," Missy said, taking her white sweater off and putting it around Julia. "Now you are all set for your wedding. Wait," she looked in her bag and pulled out a blue ribbon, "now you are all set."

"I'm so happy you came for a visit today."

"Me too."

11

"I can't believe you two got married without calling us," Rory said, looking at Kane and Julia.

Skye nodded her head. "That's what I said. I was here twice that day. I didn't get one call."

"I wasn't about to let Julia change her mind. She had already told me she loved me. I arranged everything as fast as I could."

"Your hair looks lovely. I love the short style you're wearing. Did you have a stylist come in and cut it?"

"No, Missy was here, so she cut it. Since she was here anyway, she stayed for our wedding."

"I'm glad Missy was here. Did she take photos with her phone?"

"Yes, lot's of them. Now can you all be happy for us?"

"I'm so happy for you both," Rory said, hugging them.

Skye and Lucas agreed with Rory. "When do you get to leave the hospital?" Skye asked. "I can pick you up."

"My husband will pick me up. I'm going home with Kane."

Skye smiled. "Sorry, I forgot."

"That's okay. I know all of this was quick. But I've loved Kane for three years, and I acted like a child and never told him. When I was on the side of the road dying, my biggest regret was that I didn't tell Kane I loved him. I leave the hospital tomorrow, a nurse will be there for a few hours a day. Killian thinks we should stay at the safe house for a while to see if anyone is waiting for me. I'm pretty sure there will be men out there wanting me dead. Kane agrees with Killian, so we will go to the safe house for now."

"I'm so relieved you'll be going there because I heard that Juan's son has taken over, and he has said he's going to kill you. He may have called to find out when you are being released."

"We'll leave today. I'll be right back," Kane said, leaving the room. He was back in twenty minutes. "Okay, we are going right now. I talked to your doctor. I told him what's going on. He doesn't want any of the cartels here at the hospital. We are leaving through the employee's entrance. So the nurse won't be there until tomorrow. I don't want you worrying about anything," Kane said as he took her face in his hands and kissed her. I can take care of you."

Julia nodded. She looked at Skye. "Bring me weapons. I won't ever let them sucker punch me again. If they threaten my husband, I'll kill all of them. I don't want to put your life in danger. Screw it, I'm going to kill them anyway."

"No."

Julia looked at Kane. "What do you mean?"

"No, you are not going after them. I don't want you anywhere around the cartel."

Julia would have argued, but one look at Kane, and she shut up. She saw the fear in his eyes, and she knew that feeling. "Okay, I won't go around them ever again. I promise. But I still want my weapons."

"You can have your weapons. From now on, I'll take care

of the cartel if they come around. I know everything about them. I've been studying them for ten years. You are not to ever go around them again. Promise me."

"Kane, how can I promise that? If they come for me, I have to fight them."

"They won't come for you. Here is your chair," Kane said as the nurse pushed the chair into the room.

"Here is a bag with your medications. Your husband will take you to your vehicle. There will be a group of workers getting off work right now, so this is a good time to leave. Take care of each other. I'm going to miss you."

"I'll miss you too, but not the hospital. Goodbye."

12

Kane heard someone knocking. *That would be Missy.* She was coming to visit Julia today. The nurse just finished helping Julia take a bath. "Missy, I need to ask you something before Julia comes out. I have to do a job, it will only be for a couple of days. There are some Navy Seal members here, but I wanted Julia to have someone else here. Do you think you can stay until I get back?"

"Yes, of course, I can. I still have things here from last summer. I won't even have to go back home."

"You don't have any appointments or business stuff to take care of."

"Nope, I'm slowing down."

"Really, I don't think I've ever seen a slowed down Missy."

"Well, I'm going to do it. This is my first week, so it's still new to me. I have no life. All I do is work. Polly and Zane have convinced me to slow down. I didn't understand how upset they were over me working all the time," she said. Missy turned when she heard a noise behind her, when she saw the man standing there she couldn't breathe. Her breath just went out of her. All she could do is stare. She didn't even notice he watched her with the same look. He was beautiful in a rough kind of way. He was tall and muscular like all of the Band, but he was different. He was in swim trunks, and water dripped from his broad chest and athletic body. His overly long hair was in his eyes. Without thinking, Missy reached up and moved his hair back out of his eyes.

Kane noticed, he stepped around Missy. "Missy, this is Luke Wilson. We were in the Seals together. Luke joined us a couple months back. Luke, this is Missy Wesson. She's a close friend of the Band of Navy Seals. She's also Zane's niece," he said. Kane wanted him to understand he couldn't fool around with Missy.

Luke still hadn't caught his breath. She was beautiful. Her hair was the color of the sun. Her grey eyes didn't even blink when she moved his hair out of his eyes. He could still feel her touch. She smelled like the sun aand wild flowers. She was gorgeous, and he wanted her right then. Luke put his hands in front of him so she wouldn't see how much he wanted to strip those short shorts from her and have her wrap her long legs around him while he buried himself deep inside of her.

"Sorry, I don't know why I did that. Maybe you wanted your hair in your eyes."

That sultry voice made it even worse. Luke took a step closer to Missy, and she stepped closer to him. He was about to haul her against him when Kane stepped in front of him. Luke blinked and shook it off. "It's nice to meet you, Missy."

Missy swallowed. "You too, Luke."

"See you around, Luke."

"Yeah, Kane, I'll see you around."

As soon as he was out of hearing, Missy grabbed Kane's hand and pulled him out the back door. "I love him."

"Missy, you don't love him. You don't even know him."

She started pacing back and forth in front of Kane. "What am I going to do? I love him."

"You saw him for a total of two minutes. You can't love him."

"Why is he so sad?"

"He's not only sad. He's miserable. Luke doesn't care about his life. His wife died four years ago, and Luke went off the deep end. You can't get involved with him. Zane will kill him because we all know how Luke is. He has a different woman every time he goes out. Stay away from him. At least I know he's going with me. So I don't have to say anything to Zane."

Missy frowned as she looked at Kane. "I'm twenty-five years old. I've been taking care of myself since I turned eighteen. If I want to be with a hot-looking man, I will be with him," Missy replied. She turned and stormed away and almost ran into Julia.

"Why are you crying?"

Tears, Missy wiped her hand across her face, and sure enough, there was a tear. "I must have had a moment of insanity. Wow, that was crazy," Missy responded. She looked at Kane and smiled. Did I have a crazy moment?"

"Yeah, you did," Kane answered. He smiled back at her.

"What the hell happened."

"I met Luke Wilson and lost my mind."

"That explains it. My nurse was the same way when she met him. I'm so happy you came to visit me."

"I'm going to stay a few nights. My house is being painted. Is that okay with you?"

"Of course, Kane has to go away for a few nights. I'm happy you'll be here. It'll be like a slumber party."

They both busted out laughing. Kane laughed as he walked past them. "Let's go sit outside, Julia," Missy said.

"Tell me what the hell happened," Julia said as they sat down by the pool.

"Julia, what am I going to do? I love him."

"You do not. Luke is one hot dude, I mean really hot, and you probably want him because of how he looks. But how could you love him?"

"Julia, I know you're right. I mean, who falls in love at first sight? I'll stay away from him. That's what I will do. Wow, you look great. You're healing faster than I thought you would."

"I'm taking extra care to get well faster, so Kane doesn't have to wait on me."

"That doesn't hurt your arm. Using your crutches?"

"No, well, at first it did, but Kane made this pad for me so now it no longer hurts."

"We are going to have fun together."

"Sweetheart, I'm off," Kane walked out and said. He picked Julia up and kissed her until they both needed air. "Bye, Missy."

"Bye," she replied. Missy smiled as she said goodbye, and her smile froze on her face. Luke stood in the doorway, watching her. *He seems angry. I wonder why.*

∼

KANE NOTICED LUKE WATCHING MISSY. He would say something before they returned. He knew it was none of his business, but he didn't want Missy getting hurt.

"So tell me about Missy."

"Why do you want to know about Missy?"

"She intrigues me. She kind of caught me off guard. I've never had that kind of feeling come over me before. Not ever. It felt like some part of her joined a part of me. I know that's stupid. I can't even explain what the hell the feeling was. I'll be sure to stay away from her. I don't need that in my life ever again."

Maybe I won't have to say anything.

13

"Did you read the file on who we are going to be taking to Jackson Hole, Wyoming?"

"Yes, two girls, twins at that, are going go to live with their father, who doesn't even know he has kids. Their aunt didn't want anything to do with their father. Her sister never told him about his daughters. Their mother died from a stroke at the age of thirty-three. It was caused by a heredity disease. Their Aunt Barbara said she can't raise them no matter how much she loves them."

Luke shook his head. "Poor kids. I hope their father wants them."

"How old are they?"

"Let me see. They are seven years old. They live in Colorado on their aunt's horse ranch. So this should be interesting."

Kane thought so as well. He already missed Julia. She had been doing so good. The doctor said she was a fast healer. She already cut the nurse's hours. He had never wanted to guard anyone like he did Julia. It scared him to be away from her, but she threatened to leave if he didn't keep working like he always did. Riley was always there. He knew she would call him if anything unusual came up. Riley was turning out to be the best assistant they could have gotten. They all knew they could count on her.

∽

THE AUNT MET them at the airport with the little girls. They held a sign-up that said Band of Navy Seals. They both wore jeans and cowboy boots, but their tops were different. One had on a pink frilly blouse, the other had on a T-shirt with horses on it.

"Hello, we didn't realize you would be meeting us at the airport."

"I'm sorry, but the plans had to change. I'm going to be out of the country. I thought it would be easier for the girls if they left from here. This is Tommy, and here is Becky. My name is Barbara Randall. Girls, these are the men I told you about. They will take you to your father. He has a big ranch, so I will send your horses to you."

"What about all of my things in my room?" Becky asked. "I have all my dolls. They'll miss me."

"Becky, I told you I'm sending all of your things to Wyoming," her aunt said.

"What if he doesn't want us. The man doesn't even know about us?" Tommy said. "I can't leave Juniper for very long at a time. He won't eat. Is Jimmy going to bring him tomorrow?"

"Girls, we've been through this. Please stop talking and listen to me. I'll call you tomorrow. Now go with these nice men who will take care of you until you get to your father."

"I'm sorry, Aunty. I'm going to miss you so much," Becky said as she threw herself at her aunt.

"I'm going to miss both of you. As soon as I'm able I'll

visit, I promise you. I love both of you so much. I will always love you."

Tommy tapped her boot, looking at her aunt. "I don't know why we have to leave you. I told you I would take care of you."

"Tommy, I wish I could keep you, but you know I can't. No matter how much I love you, I have to send you to your father. Now hurry before you miss your flight. I've already had their suitcases loaded. There is a private jet to take you to their destination. You take care of my girls. They are the most precious angels in the world to me."

"We'll take excellent care of them," Kane said as he noticed the pain on the woman's face. He could see how hard this was for all three of them.

"Here is everything you'll need. I have written Alexander Moore a very long letter telling him what he needs to know. Here is your pilot right now," she informed him. Barbara took a deep breath. "James, this is Kane and Luke. They are the men who are going to guard my girls. They'll stay with them until they know it's safe for them to leave."

Becky wrapped her arms around her aunt and cried. Tommy hugged her aunt and blinked so she wouldn't shed a tear, just like she promised her aunt, she wouldn't cry when they said goodbye.

It was two sad little girls that boarded the plane. Kane and Luke sat across from the girls. Kane looked around and found some tissues. He handed Becky some so she could wipe the tears that wouldn't stop falling.

Tommy kept her head turned so they couldn't see any tears. "Is your aunt sick?" Kane asked her.

"Yes, she's dying. Our mother died when Becky and I were three. It's something hereditary in their family. It has a long name; I don't remember it. Becky and I don't have it. We were tested when we were babies. Aunt Barbara thought they were wrong about her, but then she she started getting sick, and she can no longer keep us."

"I'm sorry about that."

Tommy nodded her head. "Becky will probably cry the entire flight. I promised my aunt I wouldn't cry, and I won't."

"You're very brave."

"Are you from Ireland?"

"I'm from Scotland."

"I've been to Scotland. It's beautiful."

"Yes, it is. So do you know anything about your father?"

Becky wiped her face with a napkin. "Yes, we know everything about him. We asked our mom about him when we were three, and she told us he was a good man. Tommy knows how to use the computer, and she looked him up. He owns a ranch like ours, but it's in Wyoming. He isn't married. It said he didn't have children, but he has us. Tommy said he'll want to get a blood test to see if we are really his."

"I'm sure he'll be happy to know he has two beautiful daughters."

Tommy looked at Kane."Well, if he doesn't want us, I'm not going to cry."

Luke smiled. "I'm sure you have nothing to worry about. He's your father. He'll want you because you are his girls."

Kane read all the papers Barbara Randall gave him. *If he doesn't want the girls, then bring them back to the ranch. I won't send their horses and other belongings until I hear from you. My sister told me all about Alex Moore. She loved him, but she knew she was dying. That's something we've lived with our entire lives. Shannon started getting symptoms when she was twenty-three. She had already met Alex. She left Wyoming when she fell in love. Shannon didn't want him to fall in love with her and have to watch her life fade away. She didn't realize she was pregnant until a couple of months after she got home. Please watch him closely to see his reaction to the girls. Tommy will know right away if he wants them. She's very observant for one so young. I knew I could trust the Band of Navy Seals when my friend James Mckenna told me to call you.*

Kane folded the letter, James McKenna. I should have known he would know her. He has one of the biggest horse ranches in the country. When he looked at the girls, they were both watching him. "Do both of you know our friends, the McKennas."

"Yes," Becky said. They used to stay at our house during the rodeo. "James told my aunt about you guys."

"What do you think about meeting your father?"

"I want to meet him. I wanted to meet him when I was four, but Aunt Barbara wanted us with her as long as she was able to keep us. I think our father will be happy to know he has kids."

"What do you think, Tommy?" Luke asked.

"I don't know. I have to wait and see what our dad says when he first meets us."

Luke smiled; poor kids, they were too young to know what pain was. Kids should never feel that kind of pain.

~

Kane slowed the vehicle down when he saw the massive arch with Moore Ranch hanging from it. He drove down the long driveway. The house could be seen way before you came to it. It sat on top of a hill with maple and oak trees around it. "Okay, girls, are you nervous?"

"Yes," they both said at the same time. It was six in the evening. Kane hoped their father was home. He stepped out of the car as a man on a horse came into view.

"That's him," Tommy whispered. "I saw his picture on the internet. I don't want to get out. You talk to him first, Kane."

"Okay," he replied. The man on the horse approached them.

"Can I help you?" Alex said, sliding off his horse.

"My name is Kane Walsh," Kane said. Luke walked around the front of the car. "This is Luke Wilson. We are with the Band of Navy Seals. Barbara Randall hired us to bring something to you."

"Barbara Randall, would she be related to Shannon Randall."

"Yes, Shannon was her sister."

"What do you mean was?"

"She passed away four years ago," he replied. Kane turned when he heard a door shut. He smiled when Tommy and Becky walked around the vehicle holding hands.

"This is Tommy, and this is Becky. We brought them to you. They are your daughters."

"My daughters," he asked in shock. Alex looked at Tommy and then Becky. They were dressed like little cowgirls. He smiled and walked over to them. "You must be twins. Are you my daughters?"

"Yes," both of them said at the same time.

"Why don't we go inside and talk? I bet you're hungry. Have you had dinner yet?"

"No."

"Well, I'm sure Frank can whip something up. I was going to go out, but I would rather spend time with my daughters. Can you tell me if your aunt Barbara is sick?" he said, sitting on the sofa. Both girls sat on either side of him.

Tommy took hold of his arm as she cuddled close to him. "Aunt Barbara is dying. She has the same sickness as our mama had. I told her I would take care of her. But she said we needed our dad," Tommy looked into his eyes, "Do you want us?"

Kane waited to hear what he would say. "More than

anything in the world. I would have come to you if I knew about you. I'm sorry you lost your mom and now your aunt. Maybe we can talk Aunt Barbara into living here with us. That way, she will be around people who love her."

"Yes, can we call her now?" Becky asked.

"I'll call her tonight. Tell me about the two of you."

Tommy leaned her head on his arm. "I have to bring Juniper here. He will stop eating if I'm gone."

"Is Juniper your dog?"

"No, he's my horse. Can I call Jimmy and tell him he can bring him and our stuff. He's waiting to see if you want us or not. We will also have the ranch. Aunt Barbara said you can take care of all that later."

Alex nodded his head. He felt so many feelings going through his body as he watched his girls. He went from having a life with no one important in it to having two daughters to love. He was thirty-five. His one love left him, and now she had given him daughters. His mom was going to be ecstatic. "I'll send for all of your things. What about you Becky, will your horse miss you?"

"Probably, but I want my dolls mostly. Tommy doesn't play with dolls. She knows everything about the computer. She looked you up, and we saw your picture. Mama told us about you. She loved you, but she knew she would die, so she said she had to leave you. Are you going to get a blood test to see if we belong to you?"

"No, I know you belong to me. Both of you have my eyes."

Tommy pulled his arm to get his attention. "That's what I told Becky. Are you mad at mama and Aunt Barbara?"

"No, I'm not mad at them. I wish I had known about you two, but I understand they loved you so much they wanted to keep you to themselves. Now I'll get to have you forever."

Kane noticed the panic on his face. "The girls don't carry

the same chrome in their body that their mom and aunt have."

Alex smiled and hugged them. "You two are the best surprise I've ever had in my entire life," Alex said. He looked at Kane and Luke. "Thank you for bringing them to me."

"We'll be here for a couple of days, just to make sure the girls are settled. If you can talk Barbara into moving here with you, I know the girls would be happy. It was hard on all three of them when we boarded the plane."

"I'll make sure she does. Let's go find Frank," Alex said. He stood up and took each girl by the hand and walked out of the room.

14

Julia was on the lounger by the pool, Missy was swimming. Julia watched Missy she never paid attention how beautiful she was with her gray eyes that looked like they could see all the way down to your soul. "I'm going stir crazy sitting around doing nothing."

Missy laughed. "I thought I was the only one that couldn't stay put for long. I'll tell you what we'll do. Tonight after dinner, we'll get on the computer and buy up some stock."

"Oh, I can't wait. That sounds so exciting."

"Believe me, I've had excitement and adventure, and I almost died. Just because you're used to lots of action and adventure doesn't mean the stock market isn't exciting. I promise you it'll be fun. I have to make a few calls and see what stocks are rocking it. We put loads of money on it and wait two days. Then we pull the money out. I've made a lot of money doing that. I've lost a lot as well. It's exciting because you never know if you'll win or lose."

"Okay, how much do I need? Is it like going to the casino? I have to tell you I've never been to the casino."

"It's nothing like the casino," she replied. Missy jumped

out of the pool when she heard someone shouting for Julia. She grabbed her phone to call Zane. When she looked at Julia, she had her gun out. "What is it?"

"Get my chair quick. You're going to have to get us out of here."

"What's happening?"

"I don't know. Where is Riley?"

"She had a doctor's appointment. What if she shows up right now. I'll call her and tell her to stay away."

Hunter ran out back and looked at both of them. "We have to leave now. We're going this way," Hunter said. He grabbed Julia's medication and threw a towel at Missy. He pushed Julia's chair as he ran, he hit a button, and the gate opened in the back wall. "This way," Hunter said. He pushed the button again, and the gate shut. They ran into the house and into the garage. "This way," Hunter whispered.

"How did they know where to find me?"

"Fuck if I know."

"The only one who could have said something is the nurse. They either killed her or paid her," she reasoned. Julia used her one good arm to pull herself inside of the vehicle. They heard bullets hitting the safe house.

Hunter waited until it was all quiet and tires were squealing before he pulled out of the garage. The sirens were blaring as they headed out of Los Angeles.

"Where are we going?" Missy asked.

"I don't know yet. We'll just keep going until we hear from someone."

"I'm kind of wearing a skimpy bikini. Can we buy something for me to wear? I can call it in, and they'll run it out to me. I don't even have to get out of the vehicle. Let's wait until we get to the next town. We don't have to do it here," she said. Missy's phone went off. She looked at it, and it was Zane.

"Missy honey, where are you?"

"Zane, I'm in a vehicle with Julia and Hunter. The cartel guys found out where Julia was, and they shot up the house. We barely made it out in time."

"Damn, I was hoping you said someplace else. This is what you are going to do. Put me on speaker. Can everyone hear me?"

"Yes," they said at the same time.

"This is what you are going to do. Hunter let Missy drive. You might have to use your weapon, and Missy has raced in speedway races. Believe me, she knows how to drive. Julia, don't take any chances on your broken bones. We don't want them more damaged than they are. Kane and Luke will be home sometime today. So when you get to the outskirts of town, there is a shopping center there. I want you to pull in there and change drivers."

"These people don't give a damn if there are people around. If they see me, they will start shooting and not give a fuck who gets in the way. I want to take Missy somewhere. I don't want to take the chance of her getting hurt."

"No," Missy said. "I'm going to drive. Why would you think I would let you drop me off. God, I can't believe you said that."

"Oh, really, Missy, have you been fighting the cartel? Do you fucking know anything about the cartel? I'm an FBI agent, and they scare the hell out of me!" Julia shouted. "I will not take a chance on these monsters getting a hold of you. You are going to be dropped off, and that's all there is to it," she declared. Julia held up her hand when Missy started to argue. "This conversation is over."

"Pullover, Hunter," Missy said. "I'm going to drive this fucking vehicle, and I don't want to hear another word. I can't believe you, Julia. Why would I leave you to fight these people? They almost killed you. Look at you. There is not a spot on your body that isn't bruised. Kane would never forgive me if something happened to you."

Julia shook her head. "You are impossible, Missy Wesson. Please don't get hurt."

Missy looked at her phone. "Zane, I'll have to call you back. Kane is calling. Here Julia, talk to Kane."

"Hello."

"Julia, what the fuck happened to the safe house? We saw Missy's vehicle here. Why don't you have your phone with you?"

"I didn't have time time to get my phone. Those bastards found me."

"Fuck, where are you?"

"Where are we?" Julia asked.

"We are driving on the outskirts of the city. Pull over Hunter, so I can take over the driving," Missy said. "I can't shoot a gun."

"What the fuck are you talking about. Why would you need to shoot a damn gun, Missy?" Kane asked.

"Heck, I don't know. We need to meet up with you. But I'm sure someone is watching the house and will be following you. Riley is going to Zane's house."

Kane looked at Luke. "Can you ditch them on the bike."

"Hell yes, all they'll see is a blur going by. Call Zane and tell him what's going on."

"Zane knows what's going on. We were just on the phone with him," Missy said.

"Go to the grove of oranges where we found Austin. I'll see you there," he said then hung up before she could say something.

"Does anyone know where the grove is?" Hunter asked.

"Yes, turn around, and we'll take a different route," she replied. They drove for thirty minutes before orange trees came into view. Julia looked around at the area. "See that canal when you reach the end of it, turn right and drive about ten miles. When we pick Kane up, Missy, you can have Luke take you to Zane's. The grove of trees will be the end of your ride with us. Please don't argue about it. I can't have my best friend in danger because of me."

"I understand, but I have a place for you to stay. I'm going to write the address down. It's only a cabin off the grid. It's not much. It's on the river, so it's an excellent place to get away when you need to."

"Here are the trees Austin was found in the last grove of trees. As they turned off of the road. They heard the motorcycle behind them. Kane ran up to the vehicle and opened the back door. He pulled Julia into his arms and kissed her.

"I wonder how they found you."

"It had to be my nurse. She's the only one I know of who would have said something."

Kane looked around. He spotted Missy sitting with a towel wrapped around her.

"I was swimming."

Luke walked over. "Let's get going."

Julia shook her head. "Take Missy home. I don't want her in danger."

Luke looked over at Missy. "Here, take this," he said, taking off his shirt.

Missy took his shirt and slipped it over her head. "Thank you," it smelled of his body all male and spice of some kind.

He didn't say anything. He pulled another T-shirt from his saddlebag on his bike. "You'll ride with me," he said, looking into her eyes.

Missy's heart was beating so fast she couldn't breathe. *If I get on that bike, I'll end up in his bed. Probably not even a bed, but a grove of trees. She stepped out of the vehicle and walked around to where he was. She didn't say anything, and neither did Luke. When he climbed on his bike, she climbed on the back of it. She put* her *arms around him and laid* her *head against his back. He was so warm.* She *couldn't wait until* they *stopped.* Then the vehicle door opened, and Kane stepped out.

"We'll follow you to the cabin," Kane said, looking at Luke.

Missy could have sworn Luke growled. She chuckled and never moved her arms from around him. She whispered the directions to him in his ear. She felt like she wanted to scream if he didn't do something to her soon.

"Hang on tight," Luke said. Missy moved closer and held him tighter. "You do know we will end up in bed real soon, don't you"

Missy smiled. "I can't wait. My body is burning for you to do something soon."

"I will. Real soon."

15

"What are we going to do?"

Kane looked at everyone. "We'll have to go to another safe house. We'll wait a few days before leaving. This place is fantastic. I mean, you have your own water drums. You have solar electricity. So it's not completely off the grid. Do you come here often?"

Missy was happy to be in her own clothes. She always kept her closets in her homes full of clothes. She even had something for Julia to wear. She folded Luke's shirt and put it in her drawer. She planned on sleeping in it tonight. "A few times a year. Taylor and I come here. He loves to fish. I have lots of fishing poles if you want to fish."

"I wouldn't mind having fish for dinner," Luke said, "would you like to go fishing with me?"

"I would love to go fishing with you," Missy said.

She walked outside to the shed, where she kept all the fishing equipment. "Taylor brought his truck up here full of fishing equipment. So we have a lot to choose from."

"I'll go with you," Hunter said, following them out of the house. Luke growled, and Missy chuckled.

"Missy, Zane will be here in an hour to pick you up."

Missy looked at Luke and shrugged her shoulders.

She was the first to catch a fish. They had caught ten fish before heading back to the cabin. Zane was standing outside talking to Kane while Julia sat on the lounge chair, with her leg elevated to take some of the pressure off her body.

"There she is," Zane said. "Someone is going to have fish for dinner. I brought out a bunch of food. I have to get you back to Polly. She went by the safe house and saw all the bullet holes."

"Let me wash my hands and grab a few things, and I'll be ready." *Why is everyone acting like I'm a child? I've gone all over the world on my own since I turned eighteen. Now all of a sudden, Zane shows up to take me home. I would put my foot down, but I don't want to embarrass anyone.* "Goodbye Julia, you take care of yourself. Please feel free to stay here as long as you wish. Oh yeah, I would rather have my kind of action and adventure."

"Thank you for everything Missy, I couldn't have had a better best friend. I'll see you when all of this is over."

"Yes, I'll see you then," she replied. Missy looked at Luke. "Thanks for the ride on your bike. Maybe we'll do it again one day."

"We will do it again one day. You can count on it."

∼

"Kane, I don't need to have the Band here guarding me. I don't think Missy liked Zane showing up here to take her home. She's twenty-five and has been on her own since she was eighteen. Really it was longer than that. Polly was away getting her singing career off the ground. So it was just her and her grandma. Missy took care of her grandma. It wasn't her grandma who took care of her. Missy's grandma was in no shape to take care of anyone. She had to have nurses there to help, and they were only there for a few hours a day. Polly didn't know this because Missy didn't want her to give up on her career."

"I told Zane he should pick her up before something happened between her and Luke."

"Why would you do that?"

"I don't want Missy to be hurt. Luke can never be serious about another woman. He's still suffering four years after his wife died. I don't want Luke to use her. That's why I called Zane."

"You should have let Missy decide what she wants. You know how smart she is. Have you ever known her to do something stupid? Her crazy teacher doesn't count. He manipulated her when she was seventeen and then tried to kill her. I noticed the look on Missy's face. She was not happy. This might be what makes Missy take another step in her life."

Kane realized he might have made a mistake. He should have let Missy decide what she wanted. "I do believe I made a grave mistake. I'm going to call Missy and apologize to her," he said. Kane called Missy, but she wasn't answering. "We'll stay here a week, then move to another house. Luke and Hunter left. They can get back to the safe house and see what they can find out about the cartel."

"Kane, we can't run forever. I have to face these people as soon as I'm able to walk. You know that, and I know that."

"I don't want to talk about it right now. You will have your cast on your leg for at least another six weeks and your arm longer than that. We don't have to decide anything, for now, let's get you healthy. It's just going to be you and me. I'll keep you safe, you know that. I don't want you to worry that they'll find you."

"I'm not worried that they'll find me. I don't want the cartel to kill you. Now that you are my husband, I want to keep you safe. I want to spend eighty years with you, our children, and our grandchildren. I no longer wish to be an FBI agent. I want to be a mom."

Kane got up and carried her to their bedroom. "You make me so happy. Let see if we can get started on making our babies."

"Yes, I've been imagining how we can do this. I'll show you. Where are Luke and Hunter?"

"I sent them home. I can take care of you all by myself."

"Good. Just my husband and me making babies. This is going to be fun. You can help me out of this dress to begin with."

Kane took over after he took Julia's dress. Seeing her lying on the bed naked made him hard. He wasn't going to rush this. First, he kissed every bruise on her beautiful body. He kissed the inside of her thighs, and then he let his tongue taste her. It's been so long since he'd had Julia he made himself slow down.

Kane knew what she liked. He knew how to make her gasp and moan. She sunk her fingers into his shoulders. He smiled and raised his head, making his way up to her mouth. Kane's mouth locked on to Julia's as his finger replaced where his tongue had been. Then his fingers and tongue attacked her body. Julia had so many climaxes each time, she would shout his name. Kane would chuckle, and his breath would feel like a bit of feather blowing on her most tender spot. Julia took hold of his head and pulled him up to her. Then she pushed him down onto the bed and raised herself up over him. Before he knew what she was going to do, Julia took him in her mouth. She gave him as much as he gave her. When he pulled her up to him, he raised himself, so he was on the top and pushed himself inside her. They made love most of the night. Before Kane called a halt. "I'm exhausted, darling," he said and kissed her closed eyes. She was sound asleep. Kane pulled the covers up over them and went to sleep.

16

"What are you doing?"

"I'm packing our things. We leave for Alaska in thirty minutes."

"We are driving to Alaska today? I want to stay here with you. I've never felt so safe. I love this cabin. I love the river flowing past our window. I never knew how much I enjoy being in the country. I can listen to the birds singing all day. I can make love to my husband all day and never get interrupted."

"I also like being here. But we shouldn't stay in one place longer than one month. You'll enjoy the home in Alaska. It belongs to Piper, but she gave it to the Band to use. It's far back in the boonies. So we can still make love while we listen to the birds."

You should have said that in the first place. I need to see a doctor soon. It's almost time for me to get this cast off of my leg. It's itching like crazy."

"I made you an appointment in Oregon. We'll drive to Portland, and a friend of mine will check you out. Maybe he'll take it off."

"Can we trust him?"

"Of course, he was a Navy Seal."

"And that makes him trustworthy?"

"Yes, it does."

"Okay, I trust you to know what's good for me. I'm so happy I won't have to be around all those horrible people anymore. When we have kids, I don't want them to know about that kind of stuff. Do you know what I mean?"

Kane pulled her into his arms and kissed her. "Our children won't know anything about the trash in this world until they are old enough to be told about the bad things. Now let's get going. First stop, Portland."

∼

THE DOCTOR LOOKED at Julia's cast. "It's time it came off. Have you talked to your doctor lately?"

"No, because the nurse he recommended was the who told the cartel where I was."

"That's crazy. A woman you trusted threw you to the wolves."

"Julia is related to Skye," Kane said, watching his buddy.

"What? How is Skye doing these days?"

"She's great. She has a husband who loves her and four beautiful children."

"Are we talking about the same Skye Suneagle?"

Kane smiled. "Skye Ryan, now. She married Lucas Ryan."

"You two are full of Surprises. How are all the guys doing?"

"Everyone is doing great. Austin has gone back to Texas. Most of the guys are married now. Luke Wilson and Hunter Brown joined us."

"Oh yeah. I heard Luke went off the deep end and got into

a fight with a bunch of bikers. He was in the hospital for a few months. I went and visited him. He was pretty messed up. I think he wanted to die."

Kane looked at Julia, his eyes said I told you so. "He's getting better. I guess it takes time when someone you love as much as Luke loved Susan dies. I could never get over Julia if something happened to her."

"Nothing is going to happen to either of us. So, you guys knew Susan?" Julia asked.

The doctor looked at her. "Yeah, she was in the service, Doctor Susan McGregor. She was amazing. She claimed Luke swept her off her feet. They were married for three years. She was right in the middle of all that fighting. She wouldn't leave either. I remember she and Luke got into this huge argument because she wouldn't leave when it became too dangerous for her to be there. Susan was talking to Luke on the phone when the bomb went off. The Marine she was with stepped on it. Both of them died," the doctor recounted. He shook it off. "Let's get this cast off of your leg. No more depressing talk."

"How does that feel?"

"Thank you, Doctor David Campbell. It feels absolutely wonderful. Wow, I didn't realize how heavy it was. Kane, turn your head. I need to shave my leg. It sure smells terrible. Is there someplace I can shower around here?"

"Yes, there is, but don't you want to take off the one on your arm?"

"I don't know. It was pretty messed up."

"I'll take it off and run some x-rays. Then we'll know what's going on with it. Why don't you lay down? I'm going to brace your arm up. That way, you won't have to hold it up. It shouldn't take long. I don't want you using your leg much for a couple of weeks," he said as he took the cast off Julia's arm. "Oh, I can see your arm had more breaks than your leg. There you go. I'm going to send you down for x-rays. That way, we will know what is going on. I'll have someone take you down."

"I'll take her down. Tell me where it is."

"An x-ray technician has to take her down. Nothing is going to happen to her. Stop worrying."

"Damn right, nothing will happen to her. I'll be with her."

"I swear, Kane, every time you get your feathers ruffled, your Scottish accent gets so thick," David remarked. He turned toward Julia. "Is that what you first loved about Kane."

"Nope, I fell in love with Kane when he carried me up three flights of stairs and still had the energy to stay awake all night making love to me."

Kane busted out laughing. Then he walked over to Julia and kissed her until he heard David chuckle. "You aren't supposed to talk like that in front of people. I almost pulled your dress over your head again," he whispered in her ear.

"Kane, you better back away before I make love to you right here in this hospital room," Julia whispered.

Kane laughed out loud and kissed her one more time. That's when an x-ray tech walked in with a wheelchair. Kane picked her up and put her in the chair. I'll push, and we'll follow you," Kane said to the tech.

"Is that allowed?" the tech asked the doctor.

"Yes, we'll let Kane push his bride. He doesn't like to leave her side."

"Okay, here are your x-rays. Your ankle looks good. You just need to be careful with it. Your arm is healing, but I'm going to put a small cast on it, from your wrist to right here, he said and showed her a spot above her elbow. Leave it on for another four weeks, then you should be as good as new."

17

Kane heard his phone ring and looked at the caller ID. "Hey Zane, what's up?" he answered.

"I'm calling to see how it's going?"

"Julia got her leg and arm cast off. David Campbell put a smaller one on her arm. We've been in Alaska for four weeks. I'm taking her to the hospital tomorrow to have it taken off."

"You should leave now."

"Why?"

"There was a bug at the safe house. I had word that the cartel knows about the other safe houses. They are on their way so leave now."

"Julia!" Kane called. Come here, sweetheart. We have to leave."

"Why?"

"There was a bug in the safe house in Los Angeles. Zane said they're on their way. We have to go now," he explained. Both of them grabbed a few things, then ran to the vehicle and jumped in. "I want you to sit in the back. No one can see through those windows."

"Damn, I wanted to be done with this, but I'll never be done with it, will I? What about my babies. How can I have kids if these monsters never leave me alone."

"Sweetheart, we will have children. We need to come up with a plan that will get the cartel off your ass," he replied. Kane and Julia became quiet. Both were lost in their own thoughts. Kane had to figure out how he could get these people away from Julia. *We need to find a way to convince the cartel that Julia has died. But how can we do that?* Kane thought. He picked up the phone and called Rowan.

"Where the hell are you? Have you talked to anyone?"

"Yes, Zane called. We need to find a way to kill Julia where they are convinced she is dead."

"I was thinking the same thing. I was thinking that we should have your vehicle go over a cliff. Of course, you won't be in it. Let them follow you. Julia will be somewhere else, but they don't have to know that. Come back to California. We'll do it here. I'll be planning some more."

"Thanks, Rowan. It's nice to know you're planning my demise."

"Hey, I'm only trying to help, and if killing you helps, then that's what I'll do," he teased and laughed out loud over his own joke.

"We'll see you in a week. I'm not taking a direct route; you can be looking for the cliff we'll use for our death."

"I already found it. When you get here, I'll show you. Goodbye."

Kane chuckled. "Leave it to Rowan to ease the stress. He's always been able to do that."

"How long am I going to have to stay in the back seat?"

"As soon as we leave this area, I'll pull over."

Julia looked around and didn't see anything. She leaned her head against the headrest and closed her eyes. She woke up when the vehicle was hit from behind.

"Hang on, sweetheart, they found us. I'm going to try and lose them."

"How long was I sleeping?"

"A couple of hours, there are two vehicles behind us. I want you to stay down. I'll lose them, but we're going to be making some scary..." Kane was interrupted when the vehicle behind them began shooting at them. They shot out the back window. Julia grabbed her weapon from her bag. She raised up and fired a single shot into the face of the driver. He swerved off the road and crashed. The other vehicle tried running them off the road.

"Stay down. I'm going to try something," Kane told her. He stopped, turned the car around, and then started shooting. He flew past the car and turned around again. Kane was driving straight for them when the other vehicle swerved and went over the side of the mountain. Kane kept right on driving. "We need another vehicle."

Julia took the phone and called the local FBI headquarters. "This is Special Agent Julia Sparrow. We need a car now," Julia said. She explained what happened. "You need to send someone to get these men who got away. Where can we pick up a vehicle? We'll be there in fifteen minutes."

"Tell me where to go."

"Just keep going. They'll meet us down the road. This is our chance to run this vehicle off the cliff. The FBI here can put it out that I was killed in the car wreck."

"You're a genius. Call the FBI and tell them what's happening. I'm letting you out right now. Get behind the tree."

"What? Hell no. I will not let you run this vehicle off the side of the mountain without me."

"Sweetheart, I don't have time to argue. Please just get out. How are you going to jump out of the vehicle? I can't do my part and worry whether or not you'll make it. Do you want to break something else?"

"I'll get out, but I want you to be careful. I don't want you to die."

"Sugar, I'm not going to die. I promise. Now get behind the tree. Call your friends and tell them where we are. Here, take my phone," he said. Kane had to time this just right. He had to make sure he kicked the door open, and it didn't come back and break his leg or anything else.

Julia kept an eye on Kane. She walked behind the trees until she was close enough to see what was happening. She held her breath when she saw him come around the corner at high speed. When the vehicle flew over the cliff, Julia screamed. She took off running to where he had fallen over the side. Julia tried going down the side of the mountain, but it was too steep. She was crying so hard, she couldn't see anything. Kane resurfaced and he managed to pull himself up to where she was. When Kane pulled her into his arms, her legs buckled. He picked her up and carried her across the street behind the trees.

"I'm okay, sweetheart, everything is OK. Shhh, I'm right here with you. Here comes the FBI. I need to make them understand that they have to say you died in this crash," he told her. Kane put her down and took her face in his hands. Are you going to be alright?"

Julia nodded. "Yes, I'm sorry. It just scared me so much, I forgot what you were doing," she replied and wiped her eyes with the bottom of her shirt. Then she stood up and walked to where the FBI agents were looking over the side of the cliff.

"Hello, Agent Sparrow, it's been a long time."

Julia looked around and recognized Agent Hegseth. "Hello, Pete, it has been a long time. This is my husband, Kane Walsh. I need the word to get out to everyone that I was in that crash and died. The cartel is after me. They found out who I was. I thought it was over, but it's not. I have to die."

"What about your work?"

"I'm retiring from the FBI. I'm thinking of working with my husband," Julia responded. She looked at Kane, and he smiled, then bent his head and kissed her. "What vehicle are we taking? I have to get out of here."

"It's around the corner. Here are the keys."

"We'll be seeing you then," she said. Kane took her hand, and they walked around the corner and laughed. A large R.V. was waiting for them. "This is massive. We don't even have to get a room. We have it right here. We have everything we could want. All we have to do is pull over and make love right in our bedroom. Let's find a nice place to park our house so I can hold my baby in my arms."

18

They had a big funeral for Agent Julia Sparrow. FBI agents from all over the United States attended the funeral. The old lady who cried loud and long annoyed most of the people there. She walked around listening to what people had to say. If you looked closely at her eyes, you would see bright blue eyes. Julia Sparrow was no longer here on this earth, but Julia Walsh was here to stay. She stood behind the cartel, and they didn't even know who she was.

"Yeah, she's dead alright. Joe said he shot her in the head before he pushed the vehicle over the cliff. Let's go. My family has been vindicated."

Julia let her cane slip and tripped the man who now ran the business of drugs and human trafficking without blinking an eye. He pulled his fist back to hit her, and a hand appeared and stopped him.

Kane looked down at the man, who was his number one enemy, and shook his head. "You will not touch this woman or any woman if I'm around," Kane stated. When the cartel's friends stepped behind him, the Band of Navy Seals stood behind Kane. "I would advise you to leave now, or you won't be able to leave."

The old lady cried loudly. *Is he trying to get himself killed? I swear if he says one more thing, I'm going to wack him with my cane.*

Kane glanced at her and shook his head. The cartel turned and left. They got what they came for. FBI Special Agent Julia Sparrow was dead.

"Hey, darling, let's go home," Kane said to the old woman, leading her to their R.V. They drove for an hour before Kane pulled into a long driveway.

"Who lives here?"

"We do. This is our house."

"This is our house? I didn't know we had our own home."

"You married me, not knowing if we had a home. You must love me an awful lot."

"I love you more than anything in this world."

Kane looked at her and chuckled. "It seems a little strange having a ninety-year-old lady telling me she loves me more than anything," Kane joked. Julia chuckled. Kane still couldn't get over how much Julia had changed. She laughed more than he'd ever heard her laugh. It seemed once she let go and told him how much she loved him, her personality changed. "Come on. I'll show you the inside of your new home."

They walked inside and Julia is taken aback by its beauty. "Wow, this is really nice."

"I've never stayed here before. I bought it and furnished it, but I haven't completely moved in yet. Now I can move in with my wife," Kane said. His phone went off, and he ignored it. He decided not to answer his phone for the rest of the day.

"Aren't you going to answer the phone?"

"Not for the rest of the day. Where do you want to go on your honeymoon?"

"Are we having a honeymoon? Let's go to Scotland. I want to see where you came from."

At the mention of Scotland, Elspeth popped in his head. He'd been so busy, he forgot all about Elspeth. Kane wondered if Rory talked to their sister. He would call her tomorrow. His phone rang again, and he turned it off. He took Julia's hand and pulled her into the bathroom. "Get rid of the old lady. I want my wife back."

"I'll be out of the shower in fifteen minutes."

"Don't get dressed. I have to make a quick call," he told her. Kane turned his phone back on, and he had six missed calls. All of them were from Rory. "Crap, this can't be good," Kane said. He called her back. "Rory, what's up?"

"I know you have a million things on your mind right now. I'm so scared for Elspeth. I finally got hold of her. She said she turned her phone off because this weird guy kept calling her. He would tell her she belonged to him and only him. He wanted to know who the baby belongs to. She says he scared her, so she turned her phone off."

"What? Who the hell is he?"

"She doesn't know who he is. She said she asked what his name was, but he wouldn't tell her. She said she didn't recognize his voice. I told her to call the cousins and see if Callum will see what he can find out. I'm thinking about going to visit her."

"Julia and I are going there for our honeymoon. She wants to see where I came from. She's showering right now. Is that what you wanted to tell me. I saw you called me six times."

"I was worried, that's all. Thank you for calling me back. How is Julia going to be able to hide living in the same city as the cartel?"

"I'm still working on that. I'll talk to you later."

"Okay, if I hear anything else, I'll call you. Please don't turn your phone off. Having one sibling with her phone off is all I can handle."

"Okay, but don't call tonight unless it's important."

19

Kane and Julia walked into the safe house, where the Band was meeting. A lot of them were on speaker on the phone. They all sat in a circle going over all of the jobs they had. Killian stood up and walked to the whiteboard. "We are getting swamped with jobs," he said loudly. Riley hasn't taken a day off since she started working here. I have more guys coming, but I need all of you to contact your Navy Seal buddies and see if they want to join us. I have some important news to share with you as well. Our home base has changed. We are moving our home base to Montana. The Band has bought a large home in the country there. It belonged to a movie star, so it is loaded with surveillance equipment," Killian informed them. He looked over at Riley.

"Riley's going there tomorrow. We will be looking for someone to help her with the paperwork. If you have any family members who need work, they can interview for the job through Riley. She is the one who will hire them, so it's only logical that she interviews them. Here are your files.

Read them. Our next meeting will be in Montana. That's it. Does anyone have anything to say?"

Hunter looked up from the notes he's been taking. "Yes, why are you moving the home base to Montana?"

"Because too many people know where our safe houses are. It's too dangerous for our clients and us. We can't have a safe house that isn't safe. Aren't you from Montana?"

"Yeah, I wasn't ready to go to Montana. But hey, Montana is a big state. Where in Montana will we be?"

"Bigfork Montana, it's a beautiful place. You have mountains and lakes all around you."

Luke looked at Hunter. "Aren't you from Bigfork Montana?"

"Yep, I guess I'll be seeing all the people from Bigfork sooner than I thought I would."

"How long has it been since you've been in Bigfork?"

"Since I left for service."

Killian frowned. "You made it sound like you just left from there."

"Nope, what I meant was I never wanted to go back to Montana."

"I see. I'm sorry. You don't have to go if you don't want to. We'll keep one of the houses here as well. It won't be this house that the cartel shot up. If anyone does want to go to Montana, here are the directions and the keys. Those who are leaving on a job, I'll see you in Montana."

Kane looked at Julia. "Do you want to move to Montana?"

"Are you kidding me? My dream has always been to live in the country or mountains like Skye's house. I would love to have dogs and horses. I'll start looking for a new home for us in Montana when I get my computer. When are we leaving? I'll be so happy to move away from the cartel."

"Why don't we leave first thing tomorrow morning? I still have two weeks before I need to return to work. We can start hunting when we get there. Do you need to let the agency know you are moving?"

"I'll call them. I'm still not sure that I'll go back to work. Montana, here we come. I can't

wait."

∽

"It's beautiful. I can't wait to move here. Look at that barn. Let's go inside," Julia said, taking Kane's hand. Kane opened the barn door, and Julia held her breath. There were four horses in the stalls. She heard a noise and saw a mama cat with a bunch of kittens. She looked at Kane. "Do you like it?"

"Well, I haven't seen the house yet, but I love the barn. We can sneak off and go up that ladder and make love in the hay."

Julia laughed. "The only way we'll make love in the hay is if you are on the bottom."

Kane chuckled and put his arm around her. "Let's go check out the master bedroom," he suggested. The house was beautiful. It was a new home, but the owners made it look like an old farmhouse. Both Julia and Kane fell in love with it. They put an offer on it right away. The owners asked if they wanted the horses as well. So they got the horses and the cats.

Kane wrote a check for the entire price, so they didn't have to wait long to move into their new home. They put the other house up for sale. They packed up the essentials and shipped everything to the 'farmhouse,' as Julia called it. Kane was delighted that Julia was happy. She deserved to be happy and safe. He would always make sure she was safe and happy.

"Kane, who will take care of the animals in the barn while we are gone?"

"The previous owner said he'll take care of things until we get back. I want to go tell Rory goodbye."

"Maybe they'll move here too."

"You never know."

"I can't wait for Skye to see our farm. She's going to love it."

"Yep, she will."

～

"You're right. This place is beautiful," Missy said as she and Julia walked around the back of the property. There was a path that led to the river. Julia carried one of the kittens. They were growing fast.

"I don't know why this little guy follows me around all the time."

Missy laughed. "Does he follow you, or do you pick him up and take him with you?"

"I have to admit it's both."

"How are you doing with not being in the middle of a gunfight."

"I'm always swamped with work on the farm, and I love it. This place reminds me of Skye's home. I don't get bored. Plus, I'm going to have a baby."

"You are? I'm so happy for you. This baby is fortunate to have you and Kane as its parents. When is the due date?"

"In five months, it'll be in the springtime. We want you to be our baby's Godmother."

"Are you sure?" Missy said with tears in her eyes.

"Yes, you're the only one I want. You're kind and giving, and we love you."

Missy hugged her and wiped a tear from her cheek. "I would be honored to be your baby's Godmother. Thank you."

"Tell me what you've been doing with yourself. Zane says they don't see you much anymore. You have to stay here. We are having a little dinner party."

"I realized that Zane and Polly were trying to run my life. I have never had anyone do that, so I wasn't about to let it start happening at this time in my life. I've been busy. I have a new business I'm starting up. I'm building a computer software game . It's going to be so popular; I'm looking for investors."

"Why? You don't need money. Why do you need investors?"

"It's never about the money. It's about someone to share it with. I like sending out monthly notices. And having meetings to discuss what we are going to do next. I need to interact with people. I've been living in Wyoming, isn't that funny though, you moved to Montana, and I live in Jackson Hole, Wyoming."

"What's in Jackson Hole?"

"Nothing. That's what I needed for a while. Until I figured out what I wanted to do. Now I want to ask you and Kane if you would like to invest in my new computer game business?"

"Hell yeah, I do. I made loads of money when I invested in that other one of yours. Send me the details. So are you going to stay in Jackson Hole?"

"No, I rented a studio there. I've already moved from there."

"Where are you staying?"

"At my home in Nashville, I enjoy going out and listening to the new singers. I have lots of friends in Nashville."

"Missy, you have friends wherever you live. Luke stays here in Bigfork by the way. He's at the safe house. It's not far from here. Do you want the address?"

"No, I have already talked to a few of the guys; they are

investing in my adventure. Have you noticed I call my new business my adventure? So now I also have adventures. I'll call Luke and see if he wants to invest in my computer gaming business."

"Good idea."

"I think so. Do you happen to have the number for the safe house? Is Riley there?"

"Yes, and yes."

"Well then, I'll just stop by. Of course, I'll have to take my friend with me."

"I would love to go with you, except I have my animals to feed. Now, this is what I wanted to show you."

Missy turned around and looking out over the river was a beautiful home. She walked over and walked around it. "Who's house is this? They built it around all of these boulders. So there must be boulders on the inside of the home."

"It's for sale. The people who owned it got a divorce, and they're selling it."

"It's beautiful. I don't see a for-sale sign."

"Our realtor is selling this house. She's not going to put up a sign."

"Let's go call her. I want this house."

Two hours later, Missy owned a new home. She spent the rest of her day, ordering furniture online. She turned her head in response to a noise. Luke stood there watching her.

"You bought this house?"

"Yes. Follow me. I'll show you around. There is a glass floor in the kitchen. Isn't it beautiful? You can see the river rushing by."

"I didn't know you wanted to move here."

"I'm not sure if I'll live here full time. But living here in the summertime would be lovely. How do you like living in Montana?"

"It doesn't matter to me where I live. I don't care if it's

ugly or beautiful. My favorite place is on my bike. Where I can clear my mind."

"Do you always need to clear your mind?"

"Yes."

"Do you want to talk about it?" *Missy hoped he would say something. She felt the only way he would ever let go was to talk about his wife who was killed overseas.*

"Why would I want to talk about something that hurts so much?"

Missy changed the subject. "I was going to hunt you down."

"Oh, yeah. Well, here I am."

"I have a new business I got going. I've built a gaming app, and I am offering my friends some stock in it. Would you like to buy some stock in my new business?"

"Sure, I haven's spent money in years. How much stock can I buy?"

"I'll send all of the information to you, later. I guess I better head on home. Were you visiting Kane?"

"They are having a dinner party for Riley. It's her birthday."

"That's right, Julia said something about having a dinner party. I completely forgot about it."

"I'll give Riley some stock in my adventure."

"Do you always give your friends things?"

"What do you mean? It's her birthday."

"Yes, but you let your friends buy into your business adventures. You don't need the money. So why do you do it?"

"It's never about the money. It's about the friend," Missy replied. They started walking back to Julia's home. She knew he didn't understand what she meant. How could he? Everything about Luke revolved around the pain he carried with him every second of the day. "Do you ever allow yourself to feel anything besides the pain?"

"No."

"That's really sad. And it's none of my business."

"It's no one's business. Only mine and Susan's."

"Now that is pitiful," she remarked. Missy went in to tell Julia goodbye. She didn't want to stay around where she wanted someone to make wild passionate love to her. She knew it would be like nothing she'd ever felt. But she also knew he would be thinking about making love to his dead wife. Then feel guilty about touching Missy the next day.

As much as she wanted Luke she wouldn't allow her body to have him. She respected herself more than that.

20

Kane smiled as he watched Julia running after the puppy he surprised her with. A purebred German Sheperd. If she was going to have a dog, then it would be one that could protect her. He noticed she still wore her gun wherever she went. A part of him, was happy she carried it. He wished she didn't have to worry about someone seeing her and knowing who she was. What about when the baby came? Would she still carry the gun? He also took his gun wherever he went. He hated when he had to leave her alone for a few days. He knew Riley tried to keep him home with Julia as much as she could.

"Kane, he's beautiful. Did you know this is the first dog I've ever had? That was all mine. What should I name him?"

"You can name him anything you want."

"Well, I'm not going to give him a weak name. His name is Samson. How do you like that name?"

"I think it's perfect. I don't want to go away for a few days. If there was anyone else to do this job, I wouldn't go. You know that, right?"

"Yes, sweetheart. I know that. I'll be fine. Stop worrying about me. I'm a big girl. I can take care of myself."

"I know," he replied. Kane pulled her into his arms and held her to him. Their baby decided to kick at that time. Kane put his hands on her stomach and bent his head and kissed their daughter. He talked to her and told her he loved her. Kane spoke to his baby often. He was so excited to be a father. "I'll see you in a few days."

Minutes after Kane left, Julia was about to go out when she heard a vehicle outside, she looked out the window and didn't see anything. She could still hear a vehicle motor. She took her gun out of the holster and looked at the computer screen. She brought up all of the cameras and saw the barn door shut. Julia scrolled all around the house. That's when she saw two men looking into the windows. *Who the hell are these people. They don't look like the cartel. Let me bring the screen closer. Are they wearing a mask? Why would they be covering their faces? They must plan on robbing our house. Damn, I don't feel up to fighting with these men. I'm seven months pregnant. I'm not allowing anyone to hurt my daughter. If I have to kill them, I will. But first, I'm calling to see if a Navy Seal is close by.* Riley picked up right away. "Riley, someone is breaking into my house. Are any of the guys there?" she asked. Julia grabbed Samson and locked him in the bathroom.

"Yes, I'll send Luke over there right now."

"Great, tell him to hurry."

~

KANE'S PHONE RANG. He picked it up on the first ring. "What's up, Luke?"

"Hey Kane, Julia called and said someone was breaking into your house. I got here as quickly as possible, but she's not here. Her puppy was in the bathroom. She must have put him in there before the men broke in. It looks like nothing's missing. I called the police. What do you want me to do?"

Kane couldn't breathe. He thought he might pass out. Killian slapped him on the back and took his phone.

"What the hell is going on?"

"Julia called…" the phone was grabbed out of Killian's hand. "Look at the surveillance videos."

Luke walked over to the computer. "The camera is already on. Julia must have been watching it. Let me rewind it. I see them. They have masks on. There are two in the barn and three coming into the house. Fuck."

"What? Talk to me."

"She's fighting the three. She pulled their masks off. She is fighting, but she's trying to guard the baby. She's not fighting like we know she can. Damn, the ones from the barn came inside. Fuck, he snuck up on Julia and sucker-punched her. Knocked her out cold."

"I'm going to kill these bastards!" Kane shouted so loudly, Luke dropped the phone.

"Stop shouting. Crap, I'm sending you a picture of their vehicle to see if you can bring the license plate up and call it in. I'm going looking for her. When are you coming home?"

"I'm on my way. Find her Luke. Find her and my daughter."

"I'll do my best. At least there is snow on the ground, so I can follow the tracks for a while. I gotta go."

Kane turned to Killian. "I'm going to kill whoever took my wife and child. Julia can't fight. She is carrying our baby. Who would take her? It's not the cartel. We would know if they knew she was alive. Fuck, we live in a small country town. It has to be someone who knows her. They didn't rob us. They only wanted Julia. Can this plane go any faster?"
Lord, please help Julia.

"I'm going to the cockpit to tell Rowan what's going on," Killian said.

Kane didn't say a thing. He was deep in thought. He wanted to call Luke, but he knew that would just slow Luke down. He looked at his phone. He needed to call Austin. Austin knew how to find people online. He knew how to check to see who was in the area that shouldn't be here.

"Kane, old buddy, what are you doing? Are you in town?"

"No. Austin, I need you in Montana. Are you home?"

"I'm in Hawaii surfing. I'm on my way. Tell me what you need."

"Some men broke into our house and took Julia. I'm in a fucking airplane. I won't be home for another hour. Luke is looking for her. I know you can do things on that computer of yours. If you have it with you, Bring it. I'm going to get you a private plane. I'll see you in a few hours."

"Kane, we'll find Julia."

"Yeah, I know we will. She's carrying my daughter. I'll be the one who kills these bastards."

~

KANE'S HOUSE was packed with people. The police were arguing with Riley. Kane walked over and put his arm around Riley. Kane looked at the man, who seemed more confused than anything. "Why are you arguing with Riley?"

"She was yelling at me for not doing my job. I'm doing everything I can to find your wife. If Riley doesn't stop shouting at me, I'm going to arrest her."

"Riley, honey, why don't you go sit where Austin is. He said he would show you how he looks things up on the internet."

Riley shook her head like she didn't know how to look things up on the internet. She turned and looked at Kane,

"All I said was, why are you not looking for Julia? Then he said he has men hunting for her. I said, why aren't you hunting for her? And he got angry."

"Go get yourself a cup of tea. Can you bring me one also?" he asked her. Kane looked at the chief of police. "That will keep her busy for a while. Have your officers had any luck at all?"

"Nothing. Luke called us the minute he got here. We put out a lookout for the van right away. Why are all these people here?"

Kane looked around at everyone. "Julia is an FBI Special Agent, so of course, the FBI is here. Special Agent Skye Ryan is Julia's family. As are all of these other agents you see here."

"Why didn't I know Julia was an FBI agent?"

"I don't know. Do you usually know everything about everyone who lives in this area?"

"Apparently not. I had no idea a bunch of ex-Navy Seals lived here. I will let you know if we find anything. Can you do the same?"

"Yes, I'll let you know what we find."

"Thank God he's gone. Here's your tea," Riley said, walking back to where Kane stood watching the cop leave.

Ash walked up to him. "Brinley's got some names. She's hunting for their address right now."

Kane sat down next to Brinley. "What do you have?"

"Here are three of the men who took her. They have all spent time in prison. Armed robbery and drugs, none of them have been arrested for kidnapping. I haven't brought up any address, but one of the men's parents live in the area. I'll go with you and see if he lives with them."

"I'll go as well," Skye said. "We'll take the photos of the men with us. They might know where the other men are too."

Luke pulled up as they were getting into their vehicle. "I'll go with you."

~

THEY PULLED INTO A GRAVEL DRIVEWAY. There was a tiny house, sitting back off the road. Skye knocked, but no one answered. She knocked again and an older woman answered. "Can I help you?"

"Yes, you can," Kane said. He showed her the photo of the men, one of them was her son, then he showed her the picture of his wife falling as a fist hit her in the face. "This is my wife. These men kidnapped her. This one hit her and knocked her out. She's pregnant with our daughter. She's been missing for five days. Can you help us?"

"Yes, I can. Come inside. All of these men are horrible people. My son isn't allowed around us. We got a restraining order against him. He beat his own father up and robbed him of all of our money. My husband was in the hospital for a week. Do you know how long he was in jail? One month, can you believe that. He almost killed his own father, and he stayed locked up for One month. We are scared to death he's going to kill both of us. This is where he's been staying," she said and handed Kane an address. "Sometimes he stays here too, she said writing another address down. My neighbor's son keeps track of him for us. I hope he's locked up forever. I think drugs must have warped his mind."

"I'm sure they did. You keep your doors locked. I'll let you know what happens. Don't let him inside if he comes here. Call the police if he drives onto your property. He knows he'll get prison time for kidnapping an FBI agent."

"Your wife is an FBI agent?"

"Yes, she is."

"I'll pray that you find your wife."

"Thank you. How is your husband now?"

"Follow me."

They followed her out the back door, where an elderly man sat in a wheelchair. "He hasn't been the same since he got home from the hospital. His hip was shattered, and he has a hard time walking. His mind still isn't back to normal."

"Keep your doors locked," Kane said, walking out the door.

"That son needs killing," Skye said as they walked out of the house.

"I agree. Let's go. I have two addresses. We are closer to finding Julia. They drove to the first house and knocked on the door. No one answered. Kane kicked the door in. He called the police after they found two men lying dead on the floor. One of them was the horrible son. "We called the police, now let's go to the next house," Kane said. He drove for about ten minutes, before reaching the next house. When he knocked on the door, no one answered. Kane kicked in the door. When he went through the house, he found two women lying on the floor tied up. He called the police again. This time he waited for them to arrive.

Kane looked at the others. "What do you think?" he asked Skye.

"I think someone found out who Julia is and left with her. We have to find her before whoever has her kills her and the baby."

Kane roared at the top of his lungs. He kicked the wall so hard his boot went through it. Brinley was trying to calm the two women. They both screamed when Kane's boot connected with the wall.

One of the women looked at Kane as she spoke. Her lip was split and her eye was swollen and black. She wore a long top with nothing under it. "They took the pregnant lady. He said she was an FBI agent, and he was angry because those men brought her to him. He killed two of those men. I think he will kill that lady. You have to hurry and help her. He was taking her to a cabin in the woods."

The look on Kane's face scared the hell out of those two women. "Do you know his name?"

"The first man he killed called him Rob Roy."

Brinley and Skye looked at each other. Skye shook her head. "Rob Roy, I haven't heard that name in a while. I thought he was locked up for the rest of his life."

Brinley frowned. "Hell, they are letting everyone out of prison now. Killers are being let out, faster than we can put them in."

Kane looked at the woman. "Did you hear where the cabin in the woods is located?"

"No. The woman was still knocked out. She tried to get us away but she was tied up. And when she kicked onne of the men in the head they knocked her out. That was last night. Rob Roy thought her pretty and wanted her for himself. So, they followed her home one day and had been watching her since. I heard two of the men talking. They said they didn't want anything to do with kidnapping or killing an FBI agent. They were going to leave the first chance they got."

"How long have you two been here? Look at these men. Are any of these men the two that were going to take off?" he asked. Kane was asking her multiple questions before she could answering the first one.

"Yes, that one on the floor. I've been here for three weeks. They brought her here last week," the woman said, pointing her head toward the other woman. "She doesn't talk. Rob Roy wanted to start a human trafficking business in Montana. He thought he could make a lot of money here because the place is becoming so popular."

When the police showed up, Kane and his friends left. He felt like he wanted to scream and not stop until he found Julia. *Why is this happening?*

21

Julia was freezing. She still had her boots and coat on from when she was at home. Julia remembered she was about to go out, so she put her boots and coat on. That's when she heard someone outside. Julia put her arms around her stomach, holding her baby. She didn't let the men know she was awake. When she saw Rob Roy, she knew who he was right away, but she didn't show any sign of recognition. He was on the FBI's top ten list for years until he was arrested. *I thought he was in prison. How the hell am I going to get out of here?* She shut her eyes when the door opened.

"All she does is sleep. I think we should leave when Rob Roy goes to sleep. I got a call from my girlfriend. She said FBI agents are all over town. She also said a crazy man is beating people up who claim they don't know Rob Roy, when he knows they're lying. I think we need to get the hell out of here before they find this place."

"How the hell will they find it? Hell, I never knew where it was. But I agree with you. He'll hear the snowmobiles when we start them. We need to leave before he kills us like he did the others. What about the woman?"

"What about her?

"You know he's going to kill her, and she's pregnant."

"There isn't anything we can do about the lady."

"We can take her with us. She can tell her husband, who is threatening every drug addict in town, that we helped her. Maybe he'll let us go then."

Julia smiled. Kane would never let them go. Sweetie, Daddy is going to find us. I don't want you to worry. Once these two show their faces in town, he'll find them and beat the truth out of them. Julia heard shouting.

Rob Roy was hunting for the two goons. "I'll go out first, then you go out the window and act like you were outside the entire time."

"I don't have a jacket on."

"Do what you want to do," the guy said as he walked out of the room.

The other man pried the window open. They had nailed it down so Julia wouldn't escape. *Nothing is this easy*, Julia thought. They heard a gunshot then. The man jumped out the window and ran. Julia was right behind him, except she took another route. She heard Rob Roy shouting, then he ran outside. If she didn't have the baby to worry about, she would stop and fight, but Julia wouldn't take the chance with her baby's life. She didn't slow down.

She heard a gunshot, and then the man begging for his life. Another gunshot echoed through the woods. Julia looked down, and all she could see were her footprints. She wasted time looking for some brush to cover her prints. She had to find something. She found something and started covering up her boot prints. It seemed to take forever. But Rob Roy was a fat pig. She knew he could never keep up with her. An hour later, Julia didn't realize how much being pregnant would slow her down. She had to go downhill. The only thing up was more forest.

She stopped and held her side. The baby was kicking up a storm. She must not like all the running her mommy was doing. Julia cleared her mind of frightening things and thought of good things. *What am I going to name you? I would name you Samantha, but I already named my puppy Samson. That would look like I named you after our dog, so that name is out. My mama's name was Rose. All of her friends and my dad called her Rosie, would you like that?* Julia looked up. *Mama, I'm naming my baby after you. I wish you could see her. I miss you so much, Mama. I'll take good care of her, just like you took good care of me.* Julia heard a noise behind her and turned in time to see Rob Roy being attacked by a massive grizzley bear. Julia looked up and thanked her mama for saving her and her baby's life. All of the men were gone. Julia stopped and waited to use her senses. She could smell a wood fire burning. *I must be getting closer to people. Someone is burning a wood stove.* She knew she had to find a place for the night. Her feet were becoming numb. She kept walking. Julia knew she would freeze to death if she stopped. *If only I knew where I was. At least I know the bear won't still be hungry. Kane, where are you?*

∽

"Where the hell are they? The roads were all blocked. They couldn't have left the area. Kane couldn't believe no one knew about a cabin in the woods. He drove down his driveway, and a teenager rode a bike toward him. Kane rolled his window down. "Can I help you?"

"Yeah, I heard you are looking for a cabin in the woods. I know where one is."

"You do?"

"Yes, do you have any snowmobiles? We'll have to have a

snowmobile. I found it one day when I got mad at my parents. I took off up into the mountains. I walked forever, it seemed. Then I came upon this cabin. It's way up there. Do you have snowmobiles?"

"Yeah, let's get them. God, I hope you are right. Do you know how to drive a snowmobile?"

"Yeah, I learned when I was three. I hope you have gas in both vehicles because this cabin is a long way from here.."

"They're both full. Let's go. What's your name?"

"Harold."

"Mine's Kane. Thanks for riding your bike all the way out here to help."

Harold nodded his head and moved in front of Kane. They went so far up that Kane thought they were lost until he saw the cabin up ahead. Harold stopped and pointed at the cabin hidden behind the trees.

"You stay here."

Harold nodded. Kane got off the snowmobile and ran up to the cabin. He stopped when he came across a dead man. It looked like the animals had gotten to him. Kane opened the door and saw another dead man. His heart fell. He was almost afraid to see if Julia was here. He pushed open the door and saw the window that was up. He smiled. Julia got out.

Kane ran back to his snowmobile and jumped on. "Don't look at the dead body. Just go past it. Rob Roy must have chased after her. She must have gone up further into the mountains. I see a few prints. Let's go."

It was getting dark when they saw the bear ripping a dead man apart. "That must be Rob Roy."

Kane looked over at Harold. "Don't look. We'll start going down. I'm sure Julia would start going down. If you see any broken branches, tell me."

Harold nodded. That's when he spotted the footprints.

They followed the footprints and Kane saw her running. He shouted her name, but she didn't hear him. She must've thought he was the bad guy. He shut off the motor and took off running, calling her name. He knew when she heard him. Julia stopped and turned around. She cried out and crumpled to the ground. Kane ran to her and picked her up. He held her tight. He carried her back to his snowmobile. They passed Harold, who had a massive grin on his face.

"We can't go downhill here. It's a cliff," Harold said. "We have to go back the same way we came. If Julia had kept running, she would have slid all the way down and went over the cliff."

Kane stopped. He knew there was moisture in his eyes. He couldn't help it. He looked at Julia. "This is Harold. He saved your life and our baby's life. We'll follow him. He knows where we're going."

"Hello, Harold. It's an honor to meet you. Thank you for saving our lives."

Harold had to shake himself; Julia was beautiful. His face turned all red, and he looked down.

Kane took his sheepskin coat off and put it around Julia as she settled on the snowmobile. "I can't wait to have a hot shower, then crawl into bed with you," Julia whispered.

22

It had been two days since Julia was found. Julia and Kane couldn't find Harold anywhere. "Why didn't we know his last name? How can we thank someone for saving our life if we can't find him?"

"Sweetheart, we'll find him. How many teenage boys are named Harold these days? Austin is out hunting for him."

"I thought Austin went to Australia for a surfing competition."

"He's leaving as soon as he finds Harold," he replied. Kane glanced out the window and spotted Harold. "There he is."

Julia ran out and grabbed Harold's arm. "Harold it is so good to see you again. You mind telling me your last name?"

"It's Apperson. Harold Apperson."

"I didn't get to thank you properly. If you hadn't found me, my baby and I would have died. I can never thank you enough."

"You already thanked me. The entire town has thanked me. I'm glad my brother reminded me about the cabin."

"How old are you Harold?" Kane asked.

"Fourteen. I'll be fifteen next month."

"I wanted to know if you would like to make some extra money. I need some help around here," Kane said. He put his arm around Harold's shoulders. "If you can help me out, I would appreciate it. As you can see Julia isn't able to do much with being ready to deliver the baby and all. I don't like her doing stuff on her own when I'm not here. If you don't have time after school and on weekends, I understand that too."

"Sure, I can help you. I would like that a lot. Thank you."

"Then it's settled. You can stay for dinner, and I'll take you home after we eat.

"Okay. Thanks."

"Will your parents mind?" Kane asked.

"No," Harold replied.

"Great," Kane said.

Austin wanted to tell him something, so he excused himself and walked over to see what Austin wanted. "What?"

"Harold's family is poor. I counted nine kids. Their house was spotless, but they are dirt poor. They live in a little shack on the outskirts of town. So I'm going to give him his reward for finding Julia."

"What reward?"

"I'm going to tell him there was a reward for whoever found Julia. Five thousand dollars."

"Five thousand as a reward for finding Julia, it's a hell of a lot more than five thousand dollars."

Austin smiled to himself. He knew what Kane would do. "I'll put in five, and you can put in five. That's ten thousand dollars."

Kane walked away. He went to their room and came out five minutes later. "Harold, here's your reward for finding Julia."

"I didn't know there was a reward. I don't need a reward for finding Julia."

"I know you don't, but I have one for you. Whoever found my wife got the reward. Take it, please."

"Thank you," Harold looked down at it, "twenty-five thousand dollars. "Is this right?"

"Don't you think my Julia is worth that money?"

Skye walked into the kitchen where they were and handed him a check. "This is the award I said I would give. I adopted Julia when she was fifteen; she's my baby. It would have killed me if she died out there. Thank you for finding her."

Harold looked at it, the check was for twenty-five thousand, his eyes watered, and he wiped his sleeve across his face. Fifty-thousand dollars. Austin also handed him a check for ten thousand. And on it went. When the evening was over, Harold had a total of eighty thousand dollars.

"Can I give this money to my parents? My dad got hurt real bad at his work, and he hasn't been able to work. We moved from our house into a property our church owned. It's tiny, and we kids all share a room. My older brother has a job, but when my mom buys food, there is nothing left. That's how I knew about the cabin. When my parents wouldn't let me quit school and work, I got mad and ran away."

"Harold, this is your money. If you want to give it to your family, I think that's wonderful. Are you on Christmas vacation?"

"Yes, for two more weeks. I can help out here even after school."

"What about your homework?"

"I usually do that in my last class. If I have more, I'll do it before coming over," Harold replied. He looked around at the men who were helping to cook dinner. He looked like he wanted to ask something.

"Just ask. I can see you want to say something.

"Are all of you Navy Seals? We all heard in town that there were a bunch of Navy Seals who recently moved here, and are living outside of town."

"We are ex-Navy Seals. Now we have a high-security business. We go all over the world to help people."

"I want to join the service. My mom says I need to wait until after college. I want to be a green beret. I was going to try for Navy Seal, but I'm not good with water any more. I can swim, but I fell through the ice when I was ten. I almost died. I felt someone go under me and push me up and out of the water. When I opened my eyes, my older brother was there. He saved my life. I don't like being underwater for a long time."

"Can I ask you how you felt when you woke up from being underwater?"

"It was extraordinary. I don't tell people about it because I told my class, and everyone laughed at me. My brother said people sometimes don't understand things. I died. I saw my grandfather. He stayed by my side the entire time I was dead. I know it sounds silly. I heard my family crying. I heard my brother say, 'Wake up, Harold, Mama needs you'. They were all around me. That's when my dad's health started going bad. He thought I died, and he had a heart attack. He couldn't handle one of his children dying before him."

"I told you that happens," Skye said, looking at Julia. "I know a few people who have died and seen family members. Remember Storm, he saw his grandma."

"You believe me."

"Of course, we believe you. One of the Band of Navy Seals saw his grandma. Why would you lie about something like that? What did your grandfather tell you?" Austin asked.

"He told me I was going to turn into a good man who saves people's lives. My brother reminded me of the cabin so I could help find Julia. That's why I wanted to join the green beret. I thought that's what kind of life-saving grandpa meant. My older brother said there are many ways I can save someone. When I'm grown, then I'll figure it out."

"You mention your older brother often. Tell us about him," Julia said, sitting next to him. Kane watched as she added more food to Harold's plate.

"My brother is the best person in the world. I know a lot of people think that about their brother, but it's true with Arnold."

"Your brother's name is Arnold?" Julia asked with a straight face.

"Yes, Arnold, Harold, and Theadore, my sisters were lucky they have names from this century."

Everyone at the table chuckled. "You sound like you have a great family Harold," Kane said, watching Julia pour him a glass of milk.

"I have a wonderful family. Sometimes we don't have clothes that the other kids have or a lot of food, but we have other things some kids don't have. We have each other."

"Did your brother tell you that?"

Harold smirked. "Yes, I told you he was a great guy."

"Kane, I want to go with you when you take Harold home. I want to meet his family. What does your brother do? You said he works. He can't be much older than you."

Arnold is eighteen. He graduated high school last year. He was supposed to go to college. He had a scholarship, but he told the college to give it to someone else. He said he would never leave his family when they needed him. He talks to me all the time."

"What about your father's job? Didn't they pay for him to get help?"

"No. They didn't pay for anything."

"I'll look into that, Jonah said. Who were your father's employers?"

"Okay, enough with the questions. You'll chase Harold away, and he won't come back. You'll have to ignore us. We are used to asking questions," Julia said. "That's what we do."

"Were you a Navy Seal?"

"No, I'm an FBI special agent."

"You are. Are you going to do that when your daughter is here?"

"I'm wondering that myself. I don't want to leave my baby."

"Okay, I think we should get Harold home. I'll be over to pick you up at eight in the morning if that's a good time for you."

"I can ride my bike."

"The snow is getting worse. I'll pick you up."

They got into the vehicle, and when they pulled out of the driveway, Skye followed them in her rental. Kane shook his head and chuckled. "Skye is following us."

"Yeah, and her car is full."

When they parked in front of the tiny house. It was actually an old cabin. Julia looked at Harold. "Will it upset your family if we go in to meet them?"

"I think Austin told them you all would be stopping by."

"Great, I can't wait to meet everyone. Nine children, your mother must be the strongest woman around."

Julia stood next to Harold when he opened the door. Everyone sat around a table talking and laughing. "Mom, Dad, we have company," Harold announced. Julia took over after that. She walked inside and introduced herself, then she introducedf all the others. When Harold's parents looked at the group of people, they were in awe. Seven strangers stood in front of them, grinning.

"I have to say, meeting your son has made me so happy. Not only because he saved my life, but because he's a wonderful person."

"Mom, Dad, there was a reward for finding Julia. Here is what I got. It's for you and Dad."

They watched as the parents looked at the checks. Harold's mother grabbed her chest and sat down. His father walked back over to the table and sat down. He put his head in his hands and wept. Julia looked at Kane. That's when the door opened, and a young man walked in.

"Hello. Who do we have here?"

"Theodore, this is Julia and Kane. These are some of their friends," Harold answered. He glanced at his father and continued. "There was a reward for finding Julia," he told him. Harold walked to the table and picked up the checks. He handed them to Theodore, who glanced down at the checks.

"I never heard of a reward."

"We had just announced it that morning, so not a lot of people knew about it. That's why we wanted to find Harold," Austin explained.

"We only wanted to meet you and ask if it would be okay for Harold to work a few hours a day on my farm," Julia said. "I can do as much as I was doing. Our daughter takes my strength away.

"If he wants to, of course, he can. Harold is an outstanding student in school. He gets straight A's. So I know he wouldn't let work get in the way of that. Thank you so much for this reward money. We can never thank you enough."

When they were all getting ready to leave, Julia asked Harold's mom where Arnold was. Immediately tears came to her eyes. She took Julia to the side and spoke softly.

"Arnold is no longer with us. He died when Harold fell through the ice. Arnold jumped in to save him. He pushed Harold up out of the ice, but we couldn't save him. The ambulance took Harold to the hospital, and the firemen pulled Arnold out, but it was too late. My husband had a heart attack. Our lives have forever been changed."

"But Harold…"

"Yes, Harold hasn't accepted his brother dying. He talks to him all the time. He tells us what they talk about," she explained. Harold's mother took Julia's hand. "We have tried explaining to Harold, but he goes wild and runs off. He doesn't want to hear anything about Arnold dying. That's how he found that cabin."

"He said Arnold reminded him of the cabin."

"I know. Maybe Arnold did remind him. There are angels all around us. We can't afford to get him the help he needs. He's such a beautiful child."

"Yes, he is. Thank you for telling me this story. I'm sure we will be seeing each other again."

23

Tears fell from Julia's eyes still a week after she heard the story of Arnold. She cried for him, who knew that he wouldn't make it when he jumped into that frozen lake through the broken ice. But he loved his brother so much; he gave his life for him.

"Sweetheart, are you still upset because Harold still talks to his brother."

"No, that doesn't upset me. I'm sad that Arnold knew that he would not make it out of there when he jumped into that broken ice. When is Rory coming for a visit?"

"Next week."

"Good, she's going to talk to Harold."

"I don't think that's a good idea. What if something terrible happens? I don't want Harold in pain, remembering he lost his brother."

"Kane, Rory knows how to do her job. First, I'm not going to tell her anything. Then after she talks to Harold for a while and finds out about Arnold, I'll explain to her that he is dead," she told him. Julia wiped her eyes. "God, what the hell is the matter with me. I never met Arnold, and I miss him. I can't believe he died. Harold keeps telling stories about him."

"It's because you're having a baby. Your hormones are all haywire. I have to go away for one night. I talked to Missy. She's coming in tonight. She said she would stay here with you. I won't leave if you want me to stay."

"Go, I don't need anyone to stay with me. But if Missy wants to stay here, I would love to have her. When do you leave?"

"Tomorrow morning."

"Where are you going?"

"To Oklahoma. I'll be gone for one night. I don't want any incidents happening while I'm gone. So you are to stay here on the property. I don't want you going anywhere. The snow is deep and slippery."

"You don't have to worry about me. I'm staying right here. I've never been so bored in my life. But I won't do anything to harm my baby. I'm glad you're not leaving tonight. I want to stay in your arms tonight."

Kane picked her up and carried her to their room. "We are going to bed right now."

Julia chuckled. "What about Harold? He's feeding the horses."

"Damn, I forgot. I guess I'll have to wait until tonight."

"Is Austin still here?"

"Yeah, he's going to hang around until he leaves for Australia."

"When did he get back into competition surfing?"

"He's always competed. I think he's getting bored at the cattle ranch. He says he's always busy there, but Austin is used to be in the middle of all the action. He has his dad and his brother in Texas. They all work from sun up to sundown, so I don't think he sees them often."

Someone knocked on the door.

"Hey Luke, how are you doing?"

"Are you ready?"

"Ready for what?"

"We leave tonight instead of tomorrow."

"No one called me. Sweetheart, we have to leave tonight."

"Don't worry about me. I'll be fine."

Kane looked at Luke. "Let me grab my bag."

"How are you doing, Julia?"

"I'm doing good. Can you give Harold a ride home? I don't like him riding his bike in this weather. It looks like there is going to be a blizzard."

"Sure, we can."

"Julia, don't be out in this weather."

"Kane, tell Harold not to come over tomorrow if it's snowing hard. I don't want him riding his bike in this weather."

"I'll tell him," he replied. Kane pulled her into his arms. "I love you."

"I love you too. Bye, honey. Samson, don't you go outside. I just dried you off."

∼

JULIA HAD JUST GONE to sleep when she had to get up and go to the bathroom. She felt a strange pain and rubbed her tummy. *Daddy will only be gone a couple of nights. So don't pull any surprises for Mommy. There is a storm going on outside.* Julia sat on the toilet and knew something was off. *I will not get scared. Nothing is wrong. I'm going to be okay. Nothing is wrong.* She knew when she had the urge to push, something was very wrong. It was not time for the baby to come. She still had four weeks. She grabbed her phone.

Austin answered on the second ring. "What's wrong?"

"Austin, I'm so scared," Julia sniffed, "the baby is coming. It's too early. What am I supposed to do?"

"I'll be right there. Call for an ambulance."

"I did. They said there was a blizzard, so she didn't know when one would get to me. Austin, I don't want you to drive in a blizzard. I'm sure everything will be okay. I just wanted someone to know what was happening."

"Julia, I want you to gather towels and get on the bed. If the baby comes, you want to be on a bed."

"What?"

"I was just trying to calm you. I'll be there. Don't worry."

"Okay," baby, let's get ready. Mommy will be so happy to see you. I would really be pleased if you can wait until the storm goes away."

Julia stripped her bed and put towels down. Then she put on a nightgown in case Austin showed up. She wanted to be covered. Lordy, Lordy. She felt a sharp pain, and it scared the hell out of her. She heard someone pounding at her door. *Austin, thank God.*

She made her way to the door and ripped it open. "Missy, my God, did you drive in this blizzard?"

"Yes, it wasn't a blizzard when I started out," she replied. Missy looked around. "Has Kane already left?"

"Yes," Julia grimaced in pain. She stopped and grabbed her stomach.

Missy looked like she wanted to turn around and run."What's wrong?"

"Missy, you're not going to want to hear this, but the baby is coming early."

"Oh my God, and you were all alone. Do you know what to do?" *Holy toledo, what am I going to do? I'll look on the computer. You can Google anything these days.*

Julia walked backed to her room and crawled on the bed. "I've seen a baby born once. I was undercover as a very high-up drug dealer. A whore who was high on drugs had a baby in the street. It was horrible. The baby died not long after it was born. The woman had taken so many drugs. I went home that night and cried. The poor thing didn't have a chance."

"Well, that was depressing."

"Yeah, that used to be the story of my life. Now, look at me. I'm happy my baby wants to come early, and my best friend is here to help me."

"Missy got up and started propping pillows up behind Julia. She went in and washed her hands. "I don't know anything about having a baby, but I will most definitely help you."

Julia grabbed the mattress as a strong contraction hit her. "I'll try and be a good patient. I promise."

An hour later, she didn't keep her promise. "How do women have so many babies? Their twats must be made of frigging steel," Julia said. She heard pounding at the door. "That will be Austin. Can you let him in?"

"I'm already in. You didn't have the front door locked. What the hell are you inviting killers in your house now."

Julia screamed and grabbed her stomach. "The baby is coming. Stop yelling at me."

"I'm sorry it was that drive here. I'm still shaking. What do you want me to do."

"Will you please make me a cup of tea. I could really use something to help me relax."

"I'll go do it right now."

"Thank goodness I forgot how handsome he is. I don't want him helping with the birth. I don't want him looking anywhere down there."

Missy smiled, then she started laughing so hard she fell on the bed. "You should see your face. It's all red, your hair is sticking up everywhere, and you don't want Austin looking at your twat. I swear, Julia, this is a story that will be told over and over again."

Julia chuckled, then she bit down on the towel Missy gave her. "It's going to be real soon. Can you try calling Kane again for me, please?"

"Here you go, at least it's ringing now."

"Hello."

"Kane, I'm so glad to hear your voice. Where are you?"

"I'm driving up our driveway. The airplanes were all shut down because of the storm. Why is Austin here? Is that Missy's vehicle?"

"Yes. Hurry and get in here. Your daughter has chosen right now to be born."

"What?" he asked. Kane ran into the house.

"Thank God, you are here," Austin said, relieved that Kane was there. He thought he might cry. "Hell, I don't know what to do. Take Julia this tea. It will calm her down. I'll stay in the kitchen and make coffee and something to eat. Go to your wife."

Kane rushed to the bedroom. He stood in the doorway. "Sweetheart, my love. Are you in a lot of pain?"

"Not much," she replied. They both heard Missy smirk. "I'm going to be fine, but we haven't picked out a name," Julia said. She bit down on the towel. Sweat broke out on her face. And she couldn't help the noise that came from her throat. *Damn, I need an epidural.* She may have screamed that, she wasn't sure.

Kane massaged her stomach and her shoulders. He whispered words of love in her ear. He took over the birthing of their daughter. He would quietly tell Missy what he needed. The two of them worked together. The baby was born as the sun was coming out. The storm had passed. Missy took the baby with tears in her eyes. She cleaned the baby up, and Kane took care of Julia.

When Julia woke, the baby was sleeping next to her, and Kane slept in a chair. She kissed her baby girl all over her face. She loved her so much she ached. As the tears fell from her eyes, she pulled the covers back, and checked everything on her baby. She was perfect. "Your name is Kaitlyn Rose. My mama's name was Rose. She would be very proud to know you have her name," Julia whispered as another tear fell from her eye.

Kane watched her. He loved her so much. He got up and kissed her. "I think the name you gave her is perfect. I love you, sweetheart. How do you feel."

"I would like to take a shower. Can you stay here with our baby? Don't take your eyes off of her. She's so tiny. I love her so much," Julia said. She started crying. "I was so scared something would happen to her. Thank God you came home. I want to quit my work. I don't want to ever leave my baby."

"I'm going to stay right here. Let me help you. I'm happy you are quitting your work. I don't want the baby left with a babysitter that we don't know," he replied. Kane helped her to the shower, then he lay down next to his baby. She was perfect. He thought of Austin not knowing about Ivy. *I wonder if Austin is Ivy's father.* He would find out before any more time went by.

When Julia came back to the room, Kane was sleeping, so she climbed into bed on the other side of the baby. All three of them were asleep when the ambulance showed up. Austin told them the baby was born, and she was perfect. Austin said he would have Kane fill out all of the forms when he had the time.

24

"Hello, Elie. Why is your phone always turned off. I was calling to let you know you have a brand new niece. Her name is Kaitlyn Rose, and she's beautiful."

"Kane, I'm so happy for you and Julia. I just know she's as beautiful as her mommy. Send me some pictures. Ivy, sweetie, you have a cousin. I can't wait to see her. I'm coming to the United States in two months. I miss you guys so much."

Kane told her about the big storm and him delivering the baby. "I got here just in the nick of time. I've never been happier about my flight getting canceled. Missy was scared she didn't know what to do. Austin was making Julia hot tea to calm her. He said he wouldn't have known what to do if I wouldn't have shown up. I swear, when I walked in the house, he was white as a sheet."

"Austin, I thought he was in Texas."

"Well, a lot of things has happened in the last month. What with Julia being kidnapped, I called Austin to help me. He was in Hawaii for surfing competition. But he came here instead to help me find Julia. You need to leave your phone on."

"I told you a strange man keeps calling me. He tells me I belong to him, and he wants to know who Ivy's father is. I'm afraid to leave Ivy, so she goes with me everywhere I go. I'm moving to Montana. I miss my family too much to live this far apart. I wanted to talk to you first, but if you and Rory say it's okay, I'm going to let Callum have the farm. I need to have a talk with Austin. But not until we are face to face."

"I think that's a great idea. In fact, I thought that was what I said a few years ago. Rory will be here next month. Maybe you can let Callum have it before two months and come earlier."

"I would, but it will take me that long to get my things together and shipped to Montana. I'm going to take all of my bedroom furniture. And a few other things. I'll send your bed and armoire also. Callum will bring all of his stuff here. I'll tell him to send what he doesn't want. He's going to be very happy. I've been talking to a real estate lady in Montana. She's looking for a farm for me. Maybe just horses and some sheep. I'm not sure yet. I'm so excited. I miss you and Rory so much."

"We miss you too. Did you let anyone know about the man who is stalking you? You should keep your gun on you all the time. Call Callum today, and tell him about the man and see if he can come to stay with you until you leave."

"I'll call him when we hang up. I can't wait to meet my new niece. Goodbye, Kane."

"Goodbye, Elie."

"How is Elie doing?" Austin asked, walking into the kitchen.

"She said a strange man is stalking her. Elie is going to move to the United States. She has a realtor looking for a farm here in Montana," Kane said and laughed. "She's going to have horses and sheep."

"Sheep, she doesn't want cattle?"

"I guess not. She said sheep."

"What about that stranger. Who the hell would be stalking her."

"That's why she keeps her phone turned off. She said he keeps calling her. I'm hoping that he's just a flake playing around. Are you off to Australia now?"

"Yes, in a few days. I should have practiced more. I'm like the oldest guy there."

"What are you talking about? You are what, thirty-five. I don't think that's too old to enter surfing competitions."

"That's because you're thirty-seven."

Kane chuckled, "I'm thirty-seven, and I have a daughter, who I hear calling me right now. I'll be right back."

"I have her," Julia said, walking into the kitchen. "I would love a cup of tea and a slice of pie. Kaitlyn has me so busy I'm famished. Who made the pie? It looks delicious."

"I made it," Austin said, grinning. I actually made three of them, but Riley took one to the safe house. I froze the other one. All you have to do is bake it."

"Are you a baker? I'm pretty sure this is the best tasting pie I have ever eaten."

"Yes, I can make just about any kind of bread, cakes, cupcakes, and pies. I worked in my grandma's bakery when I was growing up. My mom worked there, so my brother and I went there every day after school."

"I wish I knew how to bake. I was never taught how to cook. Except for what I learned from Skye. I was a teenager when I was adopted by Skye, and most of the time, we ordered out for our dinner."

"When I come back from Australia, I'll teach you how to make fruit pies."

"That would be fantastic! Thank you. Kane, did you get a hold of Elie?"

"Yes, she is moving to Montana."

"That's wonderful. Both of your sisters will be in the United States. Have you called Rory?"

"No, I was going to do that."

"Did she say why she hasn't answered your calls?"

"Yes. Elie has kept her phone off because she has a stalker. Some stranger keeps calling her telling her she belongs to him. Elie carries her gun with her in case he decides to pay her a visit. She's decided she is going to let Callum have the farm and just move out here to be with her family. She has a realtor hunting for a farm in Montana."

"That'll be fun. The girls can play together," she remarked. Julia knew the moment when she blew it. She locked eyes with Kane.

"What girls?" Austin asked.

Kane turned to him. "I'm sure I told you about Ivy."

"I'm equally sure you didn't tell me anything about Ivy. Now tell me who Ivy is?"

"I have to change the baby's diaper," Julia said as she rushed out of the room.

"Ivy is Elspeth's daughter."

"When did Elspeth have a daughter? How old is Ivy?"

"Ivy is fourteen months."

"Who is Ivy's father?"

"I'm not sure who he is. Elie told Rory and Jonah he was a one-night stand. She wouldn't talk about him to them."

"Didn't either of you realize I could be Ivy's father? The month's line up perfectly."

"She said she had a one-night stand on her way back to Scotland. She did tell me a minute ago that she needed to talk to you when she gets here. You have to remember you left for Texas before Elspeth went home to Scotland."

"What does that have to do with anything? Ivy might be my daughter, and she never said anything? I'll be back when Elie gets here. You're damn right we'll talk. I'll find out if that baby is mine. I will wring her lovely neck for keeping Ivy a secret. I'm going to leave for Australia, but I will be back," Austin said. He stormed out of the room but had to come back to get his keys.

"Austin,"

"What?"

"Thank you for helping Julia."

Austin nodded once and left.

"He seemed pretty upset."

"I would be angry if I had a child and wasn't told about her. Austin is a great guy. I think he is Ivy's dad. They have the same dimples."

"Maybe you should have told Austin she has his dimples."

"I almost did. But Elie said she needed to talk to him face to face. I'm assuming she is going to tell him he's Ivy's father."

"It's probably best if we let Elie take care of it. She knows when she moves here, Austin will find out if he is Ivy's father."

"Let's not think about them. Tell me more about you not wanting to do FBI work anymore."

"I've given this a lot of thought, and I want to open up a small shop. I didn't know what kind of shop, but when Austin talked about his grandmother's bakery, I knew then what kind I wanted. I've decided I'm going to open up a bakery."

"You don't know anything about being a baker."

"I'm not going to open it right away. I'm going to learn to bake. Austin said he would show me how to bake pies. I'm going to talk him into teaching me how to bake everything. I'll record everything he does."

Kane laughed so hard he had to hold his side. "You, my

darling, have completely gotten rid of that FBI woman who wouldn't think twice about killing someone who would molest a child or give them fentanyl. You have turned into leave it to Beaver's mom."

"I'll still kill anyone who harms a child. But I want our children to come to the bakery after school. I'll have them a play area in the backroom, and they can smell the goods baking as I work."

Kane turned his head before he busted out laughing again.

"I might even have a few other things in there, like gourmet coffees. I'll talk to Riley about the coffee and chocolate. Maybe even some tiny sandwiches. I'm going to name it Rosebud Bakery."

Kane bit his lip. He turned and looked at his beautiful wife, who had been through so much crap. He smiled. "You couldn't have found a more perfect name."

"I know. I love that name. I named it after our daughter and my mama."

He pulled her into his arms and kissed her. "Why are you up doing things? You are supposed to be in bed resting. You know what the doctor said. He told you to take it easy."

"I am taking it easy. I came back for my pie. I forgot it when I took off. I need my computer. I have to start planning my bakery."

25

Kane walked over to the airline woman at the counter. "Can you check to see if there was an Elspeth Walsh and her daughter Ivy on the plane? My sister told me this was her flight number."

"Elspeth Walsh and Ivy Sawyer didn't make their flight. I'm sorry, that's all I can tell you."

"Thank you, I'll try calling her," he replied. Kane knew for sure who Ivy's daddy is now. Kane also knew if Elie missed her flight, she would have called. Something was wrong, and he had a horrible feeling it had something to do with the stranger that kept calling her. He called Callum.

"Hello, Kane, did Elspeth make it there alright?"

"No, I was told she missed her flight. I think the stranger who called her has her. I'm booking a flight for in the morning. I'll call when my plane lands."

He called Austin because his last name was on Ivy's birth certificate. That proves he's her father. "Austin, I think something has happened to Elspeth. She missed her plane and hasn't called me. I also just now found out the tickets were for Elspeth Walsh and Ivy Sawyer."

"Wait, are you telling me Elie is missing, and whoever has her also has my daughter? I'm going to kill both of them!" he shouted and slammed the phone down.

Kane knew he would see him soon. He got his ticket and headed home to pack a bag. When he got home, Austin stood in the front yard with his bag in his hands. "How the hell did you get here so fast?"

"I was at the safe house. Did you get me a ticket?"

"Yes, I got you a ticket."

"I want pictures now."

"Here," Kane said, handing his phone to Austin.

Austin took the phone and sat down on the bench on the front porch. When he looked at those dimples, he knew she was his. Ivy had his smile. His heart broke because he was never told about his daughter. Why would Elie keep her from him? Now he had to find her and kill the bastard who took her. He walked into Kane's home and his eyes told Kane exactly what he was thinking.

"Her smile is my smile. She even has my dimples. How could you not know she was mine?"

"I thought she had your dimples. In fact, Rory and I talked about it. I asked Elie, she told me to stay out of her business. I told you she was going to talk to you. I had a feeling she was going to tell you Ivy was your daughter."

"Hello, Austin. I wondered if you were coming in. Kane told me you were Ivy's father. Congratulations. Hopefully, you will find her fast before she becomes frightened."

"Do you think she'll be frightened?"

"Rory is going with you. Jonah is madder than hell, but he can't stop her. I would, but I could never leave my baby, and she's too young to go anywhere." She turned to Austin. "Do you think we can bake a pie?"

"You want to bake a pie?"

"Would you rather sit around brooding?"

Smiling, Austin followed her into the kitchen. "No, I wouldn't. What kind of pie do you want to bake?"

"I have stuff for cherry pie."

Austin took out the pan he needed. He got a bowl, and looked over at Julia. "Are you recording me?"

"Yes I want to make sure I do this right."

Austin shook his head, smiling. "The best way is to use real fruit."

"I have that."

Kane sat at the table holding his baby. "Why don't you tell Austin what your dreams are?"

"I'm going to open a bakery. I'm naming it Rosebud Bakery."

"But you don't know how to bake."

"You can teach me everything I need to know."

"Hang on, you are opening up a bakery…"

Julia didn't let him finish. "Yes, the Rosebud Bakery, named after Kaitlyn Rose and my mama. I want my children to be like you when you were growing up. I want them to come to the bakery and smell all of the goodies baking."

"I hated going there after school. The other boys made fun of me because I could bake. What about the FBI?"

"I'm not going back to that kind of work. I want cleanness around my kids, not dirty filthy drug attacks or the fucking cartel. Are you going to help me or not.?"

"Yes, I am. I think you are making the best decision because no matter what those boys would say to me, they were jealous because I had a great family. Just like you are going to have a great family. I might be around here more so I can teach you other things besides pies."

"Thank you," she replied. Julia looked at Kane and smiled. "You watch Kaitlyn while I learn how to bake. That will keep your mind off of Elie. Besides, Elie can fight as well as Rory. Whoever has her will regret tangling with a Walsh."

Kane gave her a quick kiss. "You're so right."

"Hello, is anyone here?"

Kane walked around the corner. "Rory, how did you get here so fast?"

"You called me four hours ago. Ash flew me here. Did you get me a ticket? I want to see the baby."

"Yes, I got you a ticket. Okay, you can see the baby. Was there a third question?" Kane said to her.

"Kaitlyn Rose, you are beautiful. I love her, Julia. Wow, that must have been scary for you. Going into labor while a snowstorm was going on outside."

"You know I was so worried about Missy and Austin that I wasn't terrified. It hurt like hell. But when Kane showed up, all of my worries went out the window. I never knew he delivered a baby before."

"I never knew that either," she said. Rory thought that was something Kane made up to calm Julia down. "Is Harold here today?"

"Yes, he is in the barn. Are you going to talk to him?"

"Yes, I am. But not today. I just want to meet him. I feel like I want to know him. Crazy, right?"

"No, we all love him. I could talk to him all day."

"I absolutely love it here. Your home is beautiful."

"Thank you, we love it too. I guess you heard Elie is moving here. Missy lives on the river. It's a short walk from here."

"Yes, that's wonderful. I can't wait to find her. I'm surprised she hasn't escaped that man already. He must have threatened the baby. Does Austin know Ivy is his?"

"Yes, he knows. He's angry, and I don't blame him. Did you know before today?"

"No, I had a feeling he was. I wish I would have said something to him. I'll always regret that. Is Missy home?"

"No, she went to Nashville. I'll walk with you to the barn, and you can meet my horses. I want to get more. But not for a few years. When they got to the barn Harold was inside, grooming the horses. "Harold, I have someone I want you to meet. This is Rory. She's Kane's sister."

"Hi Harold, it's nice to meet you. Thank you for saving Julia and Kaitlyn."

"You should thank Arnold. He's the one who reminded me of the cabin. Arnold says everyone should do what they can for others. I love working here. I also work for Missy. She says even when she is away, she still wants me to work for her. My brother Theodore works for the Band of Navy Seals. Kane is going to help him get into college, and he wants to become a Navy Seal."

"That's awesome. Do you want to go to college?"

"My mom wants all of us to go to college. Now that we got all of the reward money, we moved into a nice home in town. And my dad is going to get some money for his accident. I imagine I'll go. But I'll miss everyone."

"What about Arnold? Is he going to college?

"No, Arnold wants to watch over the younger kids."

"Tell me about him. He sounds like a great brother."

"Arnold is the best brother anyone could have. He tells me all the time not to be sad. I'm not sad. He thinks I am because I always talk to him."

"Brothers are like that. I'm sure I talked Kane's head off growing up. Tomorrow we are going to find my sister in Scotland. Someone took her."

"Does she know how to fight like Kane and Julia?"

"Yes, she does, but she has a baby, so she has to be careful."

"I hope you find her.

"We will. I'll talk to you when I get back from Scotland, Harold, you take care. It was nice to meet you."

"It was nice meeting you. I'll talk to Arnold and see if he can help."

"Thank you, that would be wonderful. Call Julia and let her know if he knows anything."

26

Kane looked out the plane at his homeland. He missed Scotland but knew he could visit it anytime he wanted to. "Where are we going to start looking?"

Rory was sitting next to Kane. She just woke up. "I think we should start at home. He has to know her. I'm sure he disguised his voice. How else would he have had a chance to get close enough to Elie and Ivy? She also told me he called her Elspeth once, and the other times he called her Elie."

"I think you're right. I'll call the cousins and see if they've heard anything yet. I think it's someone we all know. We have to put our heads together and see if any of us can remember a stranger one of us might have befriended."

"I never befriend strange men," Rory said, walking in front of Kane and Austin.

"What about crazy Mikey?" Kane asked.

"I did not befriend him; I was his enemy if you remember correctly."

Kane frowned. "Who knows whether or not this guy isn't an enemy," Kane said. He saw Callum walking toward him, carrying Ivy. He stopped and looked at Austin. Austin walked to Callum. He smiled at his daughter, who smiled back.

"Dada."

"Yes, sweetheart. I'm Dada. He held his arms out, and Ivy jumped into them. How does she know I'm her Dada?"

"Because your photo was all over the house. Elie told her about you. She may not have told you about Ivy, but she told Ivy about you."

"How did you get her?"

"She was left at the castle. Someone walked up and put her on the steps of the castle, sitting in a deep enough basket she couldn't climb out of."

Kane noticed Austin's eyes had moisture in them, so he started talking to get the attention off of Ivy and Austin. "Did you see anything on the cameras?"

"That's another thing. Somehow the cameras were turned off. My brothers are ready to murder someone. Ewan believes it's someone that works in the castle. He said he's interviewing everyone if they look guilty, then he's going to beat the truth out of them."

"What if it's a woman. Will he beat the truth out of her too?"

Callum smiled at Rory. "No, he'll let you do that."

"So I assume we're going to the castle," Kane said, still watching Austin and Ivy staring at each other. As he watched, Ivy put her hands on Austin's face and kissed him. Austin laughed out loud.

"I love you, Ivy," Austin said and kissed her back.

"Dada."

"Now I know why you get tears in your eyes when you watch Kaitlyn," Austin said to Kane.

"I do not get tears in my eyes."

Austin laughed.

They climbed into the vehicle and Austin buckled Ivy into her car-seat and sat down next to her.

"You're pretty good at buckling baby's into car seats," Rory said, smiling.

"Well, when you hang out with Killian and his children, you have to buckle kids into their car seats once in a while."

~

Austin's eyes couldn't get any wider as he spotted the castle on the hill. "Is that the castle?"

"Yes, think of it as an enormous house," Rory said.

"Are you guys royalty?"

"Only a little, except Ewan. He's a duke. Elie is a princess, as is Rory. The rest of us has a title or two," Kane said, trying to drop the subject of Royalty. He had to hear it from his friends growing up.

The cousins were waiting on the front steps. Austin got out and unbuckled Ivy. He followed Kane and Rory.

"So you are Ivy's father. Why have you not been to visit her?"

Austin almost punched the guy, who must be Ewan. "Because I didn't know about her until yesterday. Now let's get to questioning these workers of yours," he replied. Austin walked past him and through the front doors. "My daughter is hungry. What does she like to eat?"

"Lena, take the princess," Ewan said to a maid who hurried up to take Ivy. "It's her lunchtime. We will also have lunch. It's ready in the dining room."

Austin wouldn't let the baby out of his arms. "I'll feed her. Just bring me her food. Thank you."

"As you wish, Sir."

"After we eat, we'll go over who might have taken Elspeth. I still don't know how he got close enough to take her. She took me down when we were teenagers. If it wasn't for her kicking my ass, I never would have learned how to fight," Ewan said. He looked at Kane. "Congratulations on the new baby. I understand you delivered her in the middle of a blizzard."

"Yes, I arrived home in time to bring Kaitlyn Rose into this world. You should visit us. Montana is a beautiful place to live. But no place is as beautiful as Scotland."

"I might visit you."

Rory, looked at her cousin. "I was thinking about someone who might be involved in taking Elie…."

"Why does everyone call Elspeth, Elie? She was named after our grandmother, who would be proud to know Elspeth has her name."

"Because she likes being called Elie. Now, as I was saying before, you interrupted me. Does that brit still work with your horses?"

"Yes, he does. Why?"

"Because he used to drive Elie crazy asking her out. She didn't like taking the horses to the barn because of him. He, for some reason, has always thought he was God's gift to women."

Ewan looked at Rory. "Why the hell didn't I know about this?" he asked, standing up, and they all followed him out of the castle to the stables. "Where is Doran?"

"He's on vacation. His mother is dying. He went to stay with her for a couple of weeks before she dies."

"Get me his address. His mother died two years ago."

"Do you think he's the one who took the princess?"

"Please don't call us princesses," Rory said, looking embarrassed. She knew her face was bright red, looking at Austin.

Austin smiled. "Does Jonah know he married a princess?"

"Stop it, Austin. I'm not going to talk about it. So please drop it."

"Why are you so upset, Rory? You are a princess, as is Elspeth and Kaitlyn Rose and Ivy."

"What, my daughter is a princess? Do you hear that, sweetheart? You are a real-life princess? Let me know when we leave for the man's mother's home. I'm going to finish feeding Ivy. Then she needs her nap. She keeps rubbing her eyes."

Ewan shook his head at Austin. "How is it you didn't know about your baby?"

"You'll have to ask Elie that question. I haven't spoken to her since she left the States. I've called a few times, but I figured she didn't want to talk to me when she didn't answer. Now I know she kept her phone turned off because she was frightened of someone hurting my baby. This guy will pay by my hands alright, and not one of you will stop me."

They all stopped talking when they heard a vehicle stop in front of the castle. They walked around the corner as a group and stood there as Elspeth got out and pulled a man out of the back seat. He was tied up like a hog. When she straightened up, she looked around, and that's when she spotted them. Her eyes were glued to Austin and Ivy.

"Mama."

"Yes, love, Mama is back. Ewan, I want you to do something with this man before I kill him. I have a plane to catch," she said, walking over and taking her baby out of Austin's arms. "Who's taking me?"

"No, don't let her kill me. She's crazy. Make her stop."

"I'll take care of him," Ewan said.

Callum hugged Elie. "I'll take you."

"Stop right there."

Elie knew she couldn't leave before Austin said something. "Why are you here?"

"I came to find my daughter, who you didn't let me know about," Austin replied. He took Ivy and walked into the castle. "She has to finish her lunch, then she's taking a nap. You can change your airline ticket to when we'll all leave together."

"Wait, Austin. You can't tell me what to do."

He turned with his daughter in his arms and looked at her. "You've got to be kidding, right? You kept my baby from me. Knowing she was mine."

"And that's another thing," Elie said, looking at Kane and Rory. "You know I would never have a one-night stand. Except with Austin, and truthfully it was a few nights and days with him."

"It was more than that. You should have called me."

"I was scared. I thought you would come and try to get custody. I'm giving up all of this," she said, spreading her arms wide, so Ivy will know her father. I'm moving to the States. You can see Ivy whenever you want to see her."

"You damn right I will."

∼

"You should have seen Ivy. The moment she saw Austin, she called him Dada. Austin won't admit to it, but his eyes had tears in them. I'm sure he'll be moving here if Elie doesn't move to Texas. Hell, we didn't have to do any hunting for Elie. She took care of the guy herself. He's locked up right now. So everything turned out okay. And I only had to stay two nights away from my beautiful wife. Did you miss me?" Kane asked, pulling Julia on top of him.

"I missed you more than anything," she replied. Both of them smiled when they heard a whimper from Kaitlyn. "I'll feed her in here," Julia said. She changed Kaitlyn's diaper then they crawled back in bed with Kane.

Julia yawned as she fed the baby. Kane watched as her eyes closed. A little later, Kaitlyn's eyes closed as well. He eased Julia's nipple out of the baby's mouth. She was still sucking as he put her in her crib. He bent and kissed her. "I love you, my darling princess," Kane said. He got back in bed and pulled Julia into his arms. "I love you, my darling wife," he whispered as his eyes shut. He felt Julia snuggle closer to him and he smiled.

THE END
   DEAR READER

Thank you, for your continued support. I really appreciate that you read my books. If you can leave me a review for this book, I would appreciate it enormously. Your reviews allow me to get validation I need to keep going as an Indie author. Just a moment of your time is all that is needed. I will try my best to give you the best books I can write.

Here is the link for Austin
My Book
Keep reading for more of Austin and Elispeth.

CHAPTER 1
AUSTIN

It was the last kick that had Austin flying off the horse. He felt like his head was busted in half. He rubbed the back of his head and looked at his hand; there was blood. He needed to start paying attention to what he was doing. Elie and Ivy were on his mind all the time. Austin was tired. He was sore. He'd been breaking wild horses all week, and he just realized he didn't want to do this anymore. He had no sleep last night. He hadn't seen his daughter Ivy in a month, and he missed her. It was bad enough he didn't know about her until she was fourteen months old. Now that he knew about her, he wanted to be with her. Babies grow up so fast. He didn't want to live in another State. He wanted to live closer to Ivy. Austin admitted to himself he wouldn't mind getting closer to her mother as well. The beautiful Elspeth Walsh. All of that long black hair and those beautiful emerald eyes. Her body curved in all the right places, and Austin could shut his eyes and remember how she felt under him. They had a few magical times together and made a beautiful baby girl. Right then and there, Austin decided he was moving to Montana.

Austin told himself he would stay away from Elie. Everyone called her Elie. But she would have to stay away from him as well. He knew if they were to be alone together, they'd end up in bed. They had that kind of chemistry with each other. One-touch is all it took for the clothes to come off. Just thinking about Elie's beautiful curvy body made him hard. Just one whispered word from Elie, and he would pull her to the nearest vacant room. Hell, they even did it in a mop closet at the hospital.

"Where are you going?" His foreman asked when Austin started walking towards the house.

"I'm moving. Do you want to buy this ranch?"

"Hell yes, I'll buy it. Are you going to finance it for me?"

"Yeah, I'll have Jonah, my lawyer, send you some papers."

Austin felt a calmness settle over him as he made the decision and said it out loud. *I have to find a place to live, one that is baby safe. I can stay at the safe house for now. I need to call my Dad and tell him my plans. He can visit his granddaughter and me. Hell, I hardly see him anymore anyway. He's always at work, and Dallas never quits working. He did come with Dad to see Ivy. He even sang her to sleep.* Dallas was also once a Navy Seal. He retired when his buddy got killed in front of him. He said he was tired of trying to rescue another country that didn't appreciate anything.

Austin and his brothers were named after cities they were conceived in. His parents thought that was funny. His oldest brother's name was Waco. He was married and had children. Dallas was a singer, and he was part of the Band of Navy Seals.

When he walked into his house, he looked around. This house has never felt like home to him. Maybe that was why I was always going to surfing competitions all over the place since I got back to Texas. It was going to be nice being back in the High-Security business. He felt a weight being lifted from his shoulders. He picked his phone up and dialed Kane.

"Hey Austin, what's happening?"

"I'm selling the ranch. I'll be there in a couple of weeks. I'll stay at the safe house until I find a place to live. Where Ivy can play, one that's safe for her. I miss my daughter."

"It's about damn time you figured that out."

"Pay up."

"Who's that?"

Kane laughed. "It's Luke. He won twenty bucks from me. We all had a day picked when you would move back here. Luke won the pot. He actually picked this day."

"Yes, but I won't be there for at least two weeks. So maybe Luke didn't win. Ya, all will have to decide on that one. See you around."

"Okay, we'll see you in a couple of weeks."

Austin smiled then called his Dad. He was surprised his Dad answered it usually goes to voice mail.

"Austin, I was just about to call you. I'm going to Montana with someone I met. I'm going to introduce her to my granddaughter. She's already met my other grandkids."

"Who did you meet?" Austin asked. He was a little surprised. His mom has been gone for twenty years, and this is the first time his dad has ever mentioned another woman.

"Her name is Bev. She retired from the post office, and we've been seeing each other for a year or more. Last weekend we went to Vegas and got married."

"What? You got married. That's wonderful, Dad. When can I meet her?"

"You're always so busy."

"I'm selling the ranch and moving to Montana. I want to be with my daughter."

"What about her mommy? Do you want to be with her too?"

"Dad, what Elie and I had was three unbelievable days and nights together. That's it. We had great sex."

"If you say so. Now to get back to what I was saying. Why don't you come to dinner tonight? Dallas will be in town. He's coming to meet Bev also. Another thing, I've retired, and we are moving to Miami, Florida."

Austin laughed out loud. "You are full of surprises. Of course, I will come to dinner. How long will Dallas be in town?"

"He's singing at the Coliseum tomorrow night. Then he said he's taking some time off to write more songs. He is going to be staying at your friend Missy's house in Montana. You know they are good friends."

"Yeah, that's great. Maybe he can help me figure out what to do with all of my stuff. I'm selling the ranch to Cabby. He loves this place. Besides, he already runs it.

"I still have some of your and Dallas's things here from when you were little. You might want to go through it and give Ivy something. I'll see you around six."

"Okay, Dad, I'll see you at six. I might come early and visit with you."

"I'd like that a lot, son."

"Dad, I hope I can be as good of a father to Ivy as you were for Waco, Dallas, and me."

"Thank you for saying that. You are going to be a great father. Especially since you are moving to Montana to be near your daughter. That's the best decision you could make."

"How did the moving go?" Luke asked.

"I realized I have nothing worth bringing all the way to Montana. I gave Cabby all of the furniture. He can do whatever he wants with it. I packed most of my clothes. I stored most of the things I want to keep. The rest went to the Goodwell. It's good to be back. Elie is bringing Ivy here in a little bit. She is spending the day with me. Elie said my dad and Bev stayed with her for three nights. She and Ivy love them. Can you believe my dad got married? Have you seen Dallas around?"

"Yes, he's at Missy's place. I met Bev, and I think it's great that your dad found someone. Harold has been keeping Missy's place up. He still talks to his brother Albert, who drowned when he saved Harold. Let's walk down and see if Dallas is writing lots of songs. Before Elie gets here."

Austin, Kane, and Luke could hear the music before they got to the house. Missy was singing a song while Dallas played the guitar. Most of them knew Missy could sing. After all, her Aunt Polly was a famous country singer. But to hear her belting it out was damn good. They stopped and listened.

"Damn, she's hot. I don't think I've ever met anyone like her." Luke said. "Does she and Dallas have something going on?"

"No, they are friends. Missy helps him with his songs sometimes. She stays most of the time in Nashville. Her house there has a recording studio in it. She lets her friends use it."

"Is she not as busy as she used to be." Austin waved to her from the window. They walked up the steps and into the house. They greeted each other.

"Dallas, do you know Luke?" Missy asked.

"Yes, we were overseas together. How are you, Luke?"

"I'm still here. How are you?"

"I'm good. I'm sorry about Susan. She was a great person."

"Yeah, I'm sorry too. Look, I just came to say hello. I have to get my stuff ready I have a client I have to meet. I'll be seeing you around." He turned around and left and didn't say another word.

Dallas took a deep breath and shook his head. "Wow, he's not over her yet. What is it almost five years? I mean, they were only married for a couple of years. I remember she always wanted to be in the middle of all the fighting. Actually, she wanted to be in the middle of everything. Even when they were clearing most of the people out of there, Susan stayed. A friend told me she and Luke would get into some pretty big arguments because she wanted to be out on the front line. Samuel told me they had just gotten into a shouting match before he left. I don't think he saw her anymore after that. Maybe that's it. He feels guilty because they never made up."

"That would do it," Kane said before he turned and looked at Missy. If you think you and Luke might get together, I want you to remember he'll never get over Susan. He will only hurt you."

"Kane, I know how Luke is about Susan. That's why nothing will happen between us. I wish you all would remember I'll be twenty-six on my birthday. Just because Zane tries telling me what to do, doesn't mean my friends can do the same thing."

Dallas looked at Missy, "Do you have a thing for Luke?"

Missy shrugged her shoulders. "I love him. I know it's stupid. I've never been with him. We've never even been alone together. It's just when I first saw him I fell in love. Crazy, right."

"Yeah, that is crazy. I thought I was in love, at first sight, one time. And then she married my friend."

"Was it Susan?" Missy asked.

"How did you know?"

"Just by the way, you said her name. You don't have to worry about me doing anything foolish. I don't do stupid things anymore."

Austin's head was going back and forth, "Wait, are you saying the woman you fell in love with was Susan? You two were dating when she ran off with your friend and got married. That was Susan?"

"I don't want to talk about it." Dallas started plucking his guitar.

Austin wouldn't let it go. "Did Luke know you and Susan were an item? Luke told me they got married three days after meeting. He couldn't know about the two of you. So perfect, Susan ran off with your buddy and got married without saying anything to either of you."

"That's right. I should have thanked Luke. I'm sure I would have asked her to marry me. I realized how lucky I was that I escaped marriage to her when I was out of the service and living in Nashville. I met up with a few of our Seal buddies. They're the ones who told me about Susan dying. They were still there when she died. The guy she was with was her lover, that's why she wouldn't leave. He was a married man. She didn't want to leave him behind. I'm sure Luke never knew about that. But hey, you know someone for three days. What do you really know about them?"

"That's sad," Missy said. "He loved her so much, and she was cheating on him. Never tell him this. It would be the last straw that broke the camel's back. Promise me this conversation will go no further than this room."

They all nodded their heads. They knew Luke would lose it entirely if he knew that was why she stayed there instead of going with him.

"How long are you going to be here?" Austin asked to

change the subject. He was looking at Missy, so she assumed he was talking to her.

"A couple of days. I'm here to pick up Harold. It's his birthday next week, and we are going to see his favorite singer's in concert. MercyMe, they have a concert in Jackson Hole tomorrow night. She turned to Dallas. I have extra tickets. Would you like to go with us?"

"Are you kidding me? I love that group. That's what I need. I need to watch other people sing. How are we getting there?"

"I chartered us a private plane. This is going to be so fun. I can't wait to tell Harold. I'm going to see if any of his family wants to come with us. They are all so close. So I'll be seeing you guys around."

The guys watched her leave. "So, how long has Missy known Luke?" Dallas asked.

"It's been a couple of years now," Kane said.

"Really, and they haven't been together?"

"I don't think they are ever alone together. Missy is careful when she's around Luke. Next time they are in the same room, watch her. She doesn't look him in the eyes. Even when he was talking to her. She never looks him in the eye. The first time she met him, they gazed into each other's eyes, I think both were surprised with what they felt. Hell, Luke was thrown off balance being near her. If I hadn't stepped in between them, he would have pulled her into his arms. That's how fast it was." Kane explained.

"What's meant to be will be," Austin said. "Missy is old enough to know what she wants. Stay out of her business. She needs someone too. If she gets hurt, then she gets hurt. That's her decision."

"I know. You're right. I won't say another word to her about Luke."

"Well, it's time for me to pick up Ivy. Hell, I have my own

concerns right now. I want my daughter, and I have to tell myself not to get close enough to her mom even when our fingers touch. Electricity shoots through us when we touch each other, and you know what happens."

"She's dating someone. So I don't believe you'll be touching each other."

"What the hell do you mean she's dating someone? Who the hell is she dating?"

Kane shrugged his shoulders, "She's dating the contractor who built her barn."

"Are you fucking kidding me? Elie is dating someone around my daughter."

Kane frowned. "Why are you upset about this? You stayed away from her for two years."

She wouldn't answer her damn phone. I can't see her right now. Hell, I'll wring her neck. She's cheating on me." Austin didn't know why he felt this way. *Damn, I must be crazy.* We had sex. We did not date.

"What do you mean, she's cheating. You two are not together. Besides, Ivy likes Buck."

"Buck, who would name their son Buck. What do you mean Ivy likes him. I don't want Elspeth's men holding my daughter." He stormed out the door.

"Told you how he would react," Dallas said.

"Yes, you did. But why is Austin acting like they are a couple? He smiled and shook his head. "Now we'll tell Elie Austin is dating and watch her reaction."

Dallas laughed, "I don't remember you being this way. You are treating them like you are the puppet master."

"I'm treating them like they are the parents to my niece and your niece as well. I want them to give each other a chance to get to know one another. Maybe they can fall in love. I'm rooting for my niece on getting her parents together."

Dallas busted out laughing. "Kane, have you become a matchmaker?"

"Hey, everyone needs a little help nowadays. That's all I'm saying."

Join me on social media Follow me on BookBub
https://www.bookbub.com/profile/susie-mciver

Newsletter Sign Up http://bit.ly/SusieMcIver_Newsletter

Facebook Page: www.facebook.com/SusieMcIverAuthor/

Facebook Group: www.facebook.com/groups/SusieMcIverAuthor/

https://www.susiemciver.com/

OTHER BOOKS BY SUSIE MCIVER

KILLIAN BOOK 1

My Book

ROWAN BOOK 2

My Book

ZANE BOOK 3

My Book

STORM BOOK 4

https://www.amazon.com/dp/B08Y7C9D4Z

ASH BOOK 5

My Book

JONAH BOOK 6

My Book

Printed in Great Britain
by Amazon